W9-BJZ-289

DATE DUE

Demco, Inc. 38-293

Mackenzie, *Lost* and *Found*

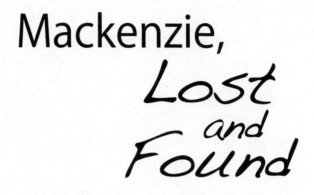

by Deborah Kerbel

DUNDURN PRESS

TORONTO

J (YA)
FIC
KERB

Copyright © Ponytail Productions Ltd., 2008

Editor: Barry Jowett
Design: Erin Mallory
Printer: Webcom

Library and Archives Canada Cataloguing in Publication

Kerbel, Deborah
    Mackenzie, lost and found / by Deborah Kerbel.

ISBN 978-1-55002-852-2

    I. Title.

PS8621.E75M32 2008   jC813'.6   C2008-906145-4

1 2 3 4 5   12 11 10 09 08

Conseil des Arts   Canada Council   Canadä   ONTARIO ARTS COUNCIL
du Canada   for the Arts   CONSEIL DES ARTS DE L'ONTARIO

We acknowledge the support of the **Canada Council for the Arts** and the **Ontario Arts Council** for our publishing program. We also acknowledge the financial support of the **Government of Canada** through the **Book Publishing Industry Development Program** and **The Association for the Export of Canadian Books**, and the **Government of Ontario** through the **Ontario Book Publishers Tax Credit program**, and the **Ontario Media Development Corporation**.

                                                      J. Kirk Howard, President

Printed and bound in Canada.
Printed on recycled paper
www.dundurn.com

Dundurn Press	Gazelle Book Services Limited	Dundurn Press
3 Church Street, Suite 500	White Cross Mills	2250 Military Road
Toronto, Ontario, Canada	High Town, Lancaster, England	Tonawanda, NY
M5E 1M2	LA1 4XS	U.S.A. 14150

For Jordy, always

Chapter 1

∿∿

The walk through Ben Gurion International Airport was long. Too long. A scrambled mix of foreign words and sounds filled my ears as I dragged my feet towards the baggage claim. After being cooped up inside a plane with my dad for twelve hours, my bleary eyes took in the jumble of people around me. There were men in tall black hats and heavy black coats, women in long skirts and wrapped hair with litters of kids tagging along behind them, and tons of hippy-ish men and women who looked dressed for the beach.

But what really freaked me out were the soldiers patrolling the crowds and guarding the entrances and exits. They all looked so young — too young to be in the army. In fact, I guessed they couldn't be much older than me. They all had long, black machine guns slung over their backs. Until now, I'd never seen a real gun before in my life. Was this really what passed for normal in this country?

When Dad and I finally got our suitcases, we stumbled out into the greeting area. A sea of eager faces surrounded us — faces searching for loved ones, relatives, and friends. We pushed our way as politely as possible through the dense crowd.

I tried to keep my eyes on the ground. The warm hugs, the cries of joy, the tearful reunions, all made me sad — I knew no one was there waiting for us. Here I was, thousands of miles from home, and all I had left in the world were Dad and a suitcase. It was absolutely the loneliest moment of my life.

Pulling our bags behind us, we walked outside through the sliding-glass doors. A *whoosh* of hot, humid air rushed up to greet me as I stepped out onto the pavement. It was almost seven o'clock in the evening and the air was sizzling like bacon on a hot frying pan.

Suddenly, out of nowhere, we were bombarded with an onslaught of taxi drivers. All were men with slim builds, olive skin, and dark, curly hair. All dressed in a similar uniform of T-shirts and cotton pants.

"Please ... please!" urged one with a big grin, pointing over to his car.

"Over here!" beckoned another. "I take you where you want to go!"

"Nice, air-conditioned ride!" announced a third at the top of his lungs.

Maybe it was because of his loud voice, or maybe it was because of the hot, sticky weather, but Dad chose the driver with the air-conditioning advertisement. As for me, I was just happy to be leaving the airport. We piled our bags into the trunk of the dirty white taxi and jumped inside.

The drive to Jerusalem was a long, winding, uphill trip. Our taxi sped along at a fast clip, hugging every curve of the highway. I chewed on the end of my little fingernail as I stared out the window. I know it's gross, but I've always had the worst habit of gnawing on my nails when I'm upset or stressed out. In the past year my fingertips have become a set of mangled stumps.

After forty-five minutes we arrived in a city filled with buildings, people, and busyness. Suddenly, there was so much to see: buses everywhere, little boys playing soccer in the streets, women wearing head scarves toting their babies and shopping bags, soldiers standing guard in front of every store, and buildings so much older than any I'd ever seen back in Canada. They even had graffiti here, too, although I couldn't tell if the words were written in Hebrew or Arabic.

Our taxi zipped through the streets, which had narrowed and grown increasingly winding. Horns were honking from every direction as drivers, who seemed high on aggression and low on patience, flew by at breakneck speeds. I started to feel dizzy as the car darted around sharp corners and through tiny gaps in traffic. A couple of times I had to close my eyes as the driver negotiated our taxi through a space that looked much too tight. Somehow, however, he managed to get us through each time without a scratch. After a particularly sharp turn, Dad leaned over and whispered, "Different from home, isn't it?"

That was probably the understatement of the century. This place was *nothing* like home. I nodded slightly and held my stomach, praying I wouldn't throw up.

I felt like an alien who'd just landed on a strange planet. Even my body signals were confused. Although I knew it was technically evening, it didn't feel like it. I'd lost all sense of time up in that plane. Now I didn't know if I should be hungry or thirsty, sleepy or awake. I took a deep breath and thought about the return airline ticket tucked away in the bottom of my suitcase. Dad had promised that I could go back home to Toronto if

I hated it here after three months. It was the only way he'd been able to get me on that plane.

A moment later, he leaned forward and gave the driver an address.

"Is that where we're going to live?" I asked.

"Yeah, I got us an apartment in a nice family neighbourhood near the university," he replied. "Apparently a lot of the faculty live in the area. It's called French Hill."

"French Hill," I repeated under my breath. I liked the name of the place. It sounded almost familiar, like a neighbourhood you might find in Canada.

But it didn't look at all like Canada when we arrived. The taxi pulled up at an apartment building on a quiet street, set a bit back from the main road. Surrounded by olive and lemon trees, the building was made from large blocks of bumpy, dust-coloured stone. Nothing at all like the red and brown brick buildings I was used to back in Toronto.

"That's Jerusalem Stone," explained Dad, noticing me staring. "They chop it right out of the ground near the Jordan River. By law, every structure in Jerusalem must be built with it."

I nodded and opened the taxi door. The instant I stepped out, an overwhelming aroma of spice and frying oil wafted under my nose. Jerusalem definitely didn't smell like Canada, either!

Dad paid the driver and we walked into the building, dragging our bags behind us. The first thing I noticed was the list of tenants on the apartment mailboxes.

"Har-Zahav ... Ben-Shahar ... Yedidyah ... Zahavy ... Machuv ... Azoulay," I whispered under my breath, sounding them out slowly. Each one of them was a tongue twister.

"So where to now, Dad?" I asked, glancing around the rest of the lobby, half-hoping there would be another Canadian from the university there to greet us. But the only other person in the lobby was a middle-aged woman puffing away on a cigarette — even though it was clear from the signs that this was a non-smoking building. I tried to breathe through my mouth so I wouldn't smell her stinky cloud of smoke, but it didn't work. Christina and I tried smoking a couple of years ago. Back then, I thought smoking a cigarette would be glamorous and very grown-up. But it didn't feel that way at all. In fact, after three puffs, I ended up with my head over the toilet talking to Ralph on the big white telephone. Pretty glamorous, huh? And ever since then the smell of smoke grosses me out.

Dad rummaged through his pockets and pulled out a folded envelope. Inside was a key chain and a small piece of paper.

"Says here that we're on the top floor," he said, walking over and pushing the button for the elevator. We rode it up to the top, which didn't take very long since there were only four floors in the building. It felt weird riding an elevator to my home; until this moment, I'd always lived in a house.

At door number 403, Dad turned the key in the lock and we stepped inside. Instantly, a feeling of relief came over me. Finally, here was something that reminded me a bit of home — Nana Pearl's condo back in Toronto, to be specific. Like Nana's, the furniture was a mix of modern pieces and older antiques. And, like Nana's, the space was roomy and open — more than enough for two people to live comfortably.

I dropped my bag in the front hall and ventured further in. There was a small television set at one end of the living room and an upright piano at the other. On the wall in between, an arched wicker bookshelf housed a collection of paperbacks, which, I was relieved to find, were all in English. The floors were covered in tile instead of carpet or hardwood. Despite the dark furniture, however, the place was pleasantly bright with rays of soft evening light streaming in through the windows. And thankfully, there was air conditioning.

I wandered further and found the kitchen. The appliances looked new but there was less floor and counter space than what I'd been used to at home. And the oven was the tiniest I'd ever seen. *How can anybody roast a Christmas turkey in that?* I opened up the cupboards and peeked inside; they were bare but clean. I closed them up again and thought about my old kitchen in Toronto. In the past year I'd pretty much taken over the cooking duties. On Dad's nights, we just ordered pizza. In the beginning, I hadn't really minded. But after a year, I was sick of it. When the delivery guy starts to feel like a member of the family, you know you've got problems. Every time he rang our bell, it reminded me of how alone Dad and I were.

It was in that kitchen back home, three months ago almost to the day, that Dad had dropped the bombshell about Israel. I'd known something was wrong when I found him chopping vegetables for a tomato sauce.

"What are you doing? It's my turn to do dinner tonight," I reminded him, pointing to the calendar of household chores that hung on the fridge.

But he just smiled mysteriously and kept chopping. Actually, it was more like hacking.

"I know you're getting tired of all those pizzas, so I thought I'd try making something myself. And actually, I have a bit of exciting news."

News?

I sat down on the nearest chair and waited. I could tell by the tone of his voice that it was going to be big.

"I've been offered a prestigious honour at work," he began. "Something I've been dreaming about most of my career. It's a visiting professorship at The Hebrew University in Jerusalem for the coming school year. I'm going to be the associate director of the continuing excavation in Tiberias."

My jaw dropped open. "Um, what exactly does it mean?" I could feel the muscles in my chest begin to tighten up — somehow I knew his answer wouldn't be good.

Dad put down the chopping knife and reached for my hand. "Honey, it means that, as of July, we'll be moving to Israel."

"What?" I gasped, staring at him as if he'd just announced that we were re-locating to the moon. "Who? You and me?"

"That's right," he replied, his smile fading fast, "I ... I was hoping you'd be surprised!"

I shut my eyes for a second and tried to make some sense out of what I was hearing. When I opened them again, I could tell by the deep frown lines on his forehead that this wasn't a joke.

"No! We can't go to Israel!" I said, yanking my hand away. "We're Canadians! *This* is our home!"

"Of course this is our home," he said gently, "but saying no to an honour like this would be like turning down the Nobel Prize. Anyway, travelling to a new place is an adventure. It's only for a year. I thought this would be a great opportunity for us."

I felt like screaming, *An adventure? Are you crazy?* But when I opened my mouth, no words came out. My chest was getting tighter and tighter — it was getting hard to breathe, let alone talk.

Until that moment my entire religious experience had been limited to Santa Claus, the Easter Bunny, and a couple visits to Christina Georgas's Greek Orthodox Church. What on earth would we do in Israel?

"But Dad," I finally managed to squeak out, "we're not religious at all! We're not even Jewish! Why do you want to go there?"

He waved away my concerns.

"You don't have to be Jewish to live in Jerusalem. It's considered the centre of many different religions.

And the opportunities for archaeological study are tremendous! Tiberias is a fascinating place, Mack: an ancient city where Jesus preached back in Biblical times. And the team in Israel is hoping I can help them uncover signs of Herod's palace. Just imagine ... I might help to discover one of the greatest archaeological treasures in history. You can even help on the dig if you want — it'll be exciting!"

Herod's palace? Unearthed antiquities? Exciting?

"You can't make me, Dad. I ... I won't go!"

He took a deep breath, as if he needed to gather his strength before continuing.

"Oh yes you will, honey," he replied. Although his voice was quiet, his tone made it clear there was no room for debate. "Can't you see how badly we need to get away from this place? You and I are all we have left in this world and, damn it, we do things together!"

His words stabbed at my heart. I couldn't believe what was happening. I felt like I'd been dropped into a speeding car that was about to drive off the edge of a steep cliff. Suddenly, my mind started swirling with violent little snippets I'd seen on the news about Israel: bombings, uprisings, terrorism, rocket attacks. Just the thought of moving there raised a swarm of goosebumps on my arms and legs. For the past year, I'd been paranoid about dying a sudden, violent death — like it was my genetic destiny or something. And Dad wanted to move us to the Middle East? No way, we couldn't move there!

But we did. Despite all my protests, our old kitchen and our old home were sold out from under me.

And now, here we were in a new home, and Dad was looking at me anxiously.

"So, what do you think?" he asked, his voice rising with hope. It was a loaded question. From the look on his face, I knew he wasn't just asking about the apartment. He was asking what I thought about the entire deal: the country, the people, the whole new life he'd arranged for us. Spinning around on my heel, I ignored his question and wandered off to look at the rest of the apartment.

"Which room's mine?" I asked, opening up doors. The first one I tried looked like a linen closet and the second one was a bathroom, which immediately reminded me of how badly I had to go.

"Excuse me for a second," I said, shutting the door behind me. "I'll be right back."

After doing my business, I pulled up my pants, washed my hands, and turned around to flush.

"Huh?" I said, staring down at the pair of buttons on top of the toilet.

"Um ... Dad ... I think I need some help in here!"

He opened the door and peeked inside.

"What is it, honey?"

When he saw me standing over the toilet, a look of understanding flickered across his face and he started chuckling.

"That's okay, I read about this, too. You see, here, lots of Israeli toilets have two flushers, the smaller of which uses the lesser volume of water needed to clear out a 'number one.' In other words, that's a half flush for urine and a full flush for ..."

"*Okay* Dad!" I interrupted. "Thank you very much — I get the picture!"

As my face turned red, I pushed the smaller button and walked out. Dad followed behind, all the while explaining Israel's brilliant technological feats.

"They're very advanced in a lot of different areas: science, cancer research, military technology, and, naturally, water conservation, being in the desert and all. It can get extremely dry here; there are times when the very religious pray for rain."

Gee, sounds pretty technical there! Do they use voodoo dolls as well?

"Dad, you're lecturing again," I interrupted. "And

it's been a long trip. I'm exhausted and I think I need to lie down."

"Of course, Mack. I don't know what I was thinking," he said, opening up the door directly across the hall from the bathroom. "I think this one's your room. You have a nice rest."

He reached out to give me a hug, but I stiffened at his touch. A look of hurt flashed across his face. I felt a small twinge of pity for him as he walked away. As wrapped up as I'd been in my own problems, I sometimes forgot that the past year had been hard for him, too. But I squashed that twinge before it got any stronger. I just couldn't feel sorry for someone who was ruining my life.

With a heavy sigh, I closed the door behind me and took a quick look around my new room. It was pretty plain. There was a wooden dresser, a mirror, and a double bed covered with an ugly flowered blanket. A wide window across from the bed offered a view of the surrounding hills and the busy intersection below.

I kicked off my shoes and collapsed onto the bed. Right now, all I wanted to do was rest. I couldn't remember ever feeling so exhausted. It was like a truck had run me over once and then backed up to finish the job.

As I lay in bed waiting for sleep to come, images from the day passed through my mind. The bearded men in the airport ... the smoker in the lobby ... the head-scarved women with their babies ... the soldiers. It was all so different. And yet, in a weird way, it was also kind of nice. Nobody here felt sorry for me. For the first time in a year, I didn't feel pitied.

Maybe we did need to get away for a bit, I thought with a yawn. *And it's only for three months, after all.*

Chapter 2

ᴧᴧ

My body clock was *totally* messed up. I woke up the next morning before sunrise and, as hard as I tried, I couldn't get back to sleep. So instead I began to unpack my suitcase and scatter some of my personal stuff around the room. My diary, my yearbook, and my yellow stuffed Frou-frou bear — a favourite toy left over from childhood — all found a home on the little shelf next to the bed.

Ah, Frou-frou! When I was little, he had literally been my best friend. For years I'd slept with him, confided in him, and taken him everywhere I went. Now, with his fur worn and tattered and one of his ears missing, he had made the journey to Jerusalem with me. Even though I was almost fifteen now, I really couldn't imagine any house ever being a home without my Frou-frou.

The next thing I unpacked was Mom's old cashmere sweater. I hugged it close, letting the memory of her soft touch take over. I missed her so much. For the millionth time, I found myself wishing that our lives didn't have to be this way — that everything could go back to normal.

The last thing to come out of my suitcase was a framed picture of Mom taken the summer I turned thirteen. Even though her eyes were squinting slightly in the sunlight, it was a great photo. She was laughing at a joke I'd made right before I clicked the shutter. Although I couldn't remember what the joke was now, the rest of the moment was still so vivid in my mind. The two of us had been eating Popsicles and relaxing in the backyard on a hot weekend afternoon in August. I had been playing around with the new digital camera I'd gotten for my birthday and Mom had volunteered to be my model. Of all the photos I'd taken that day, I remember thinking that this one captured Mom's personality the best. Her eyes were lit up with joy, her mouth was slightly red from the cherry-flavoured Popsicle, the sun was shining through her brown hair like a halo, and the smile on her face was easy and natural and so happy.

Back home in Toronto, I'd kept the picture in my nightstand drawer, tucked under a book where I didn't have to face the pain of looking at it every day. Now, I held it tenderly in my hands while I contemplated where to put it in my new room.

Mom's eyes stared up at me from beneath the glass. *Ouch.*

I folded Mom's sweater carefully around the picture, opened my new nightstand drawer, and slid them both inside. After that, I took some time to look around my new home. One by one, I examined all the books on the wicker shelf. I tried out all the appliances, making sure each one of them was in working order. I flipped on the television set, surfing the channels for something — anything — that looked familiar.

And then I walked down the hall and found the bomb shelter.

It was a small room at the end of the hall about the size of a powder room. There was one window, which was sealed and covered in a thick plastic curtain. In addition to a couple of cases of bottled water and a folding chair, the owners had left a trio of gas masks, more plastic sheeting, and a roll of duct tape. I quickly figured out these were to be used in the event of a poisonous gas attack. There was a sign on the door with instructions in both English and Hebrew:

<u>In Case of Emergency</u>
Bring radio into shelter.
Ensure there is one gas mask for
every person in shelter.
Seal door edges with thick strips of
tape once bomb shelter is closed.
Seal the bottom of door with
a wet towel.
Do <u>not</u> leave until you hear the
"all-clear" signal.

Holy crap! The whole idea of a bomb shelter was frigging creepy. The air was stale and claustrophobic and the gas masks looked like lifeless alien faces lying there on the floor.

Later on, when I showed the room to Dad, he did his best to downplay it.

"Don't worry about it, Mack," he said, waving off my concerns like a pesky fly. "Every house and apartment in Israel is required to have one of these things. It's like, I don't know ... seat belts in a car ... or emergency exits in a movie theatre ... or fire extinguishers in school classrooms. Just something that's required by law for safety reasons."

I rolled my eyes in disgust and wondered for the millionth time why he'd brought us here.

Yeah, right, Dad. A bomb shelter is no different than an exit sign!

How could I have known that one day I'd actually have to use it?

The next morning, Dad and I were given an orientation tour of the university by one of his new colleagues in the Institute of Archaeology.

"Hi, I'm Professor Anderson," she said, shaking our hands and grinning widely. "But please call me Sharon. I'm the resident pottery specialist here at Hebrew U — although I'm originally from the University of Minnesota. I guess that's not too far from your neck of the woods — relatively speaking."

I liked her instantly. With her girlish blond ponytail and freckled cheeks, she looked far too young and pretty to be a professor, let alone an archaeologist. In fact, she didn't look much older than a student herself. It was a big contrast to Dad's colleagues back home, who had all seemed as old and dry as a bunch of prehistoric fossils.

Sharon led us around the grounds, pointing out the requisite places of interest. But for me, the best part of the tour wasn't the buildings or the library; it was her advice about living in Israel.

"I know you guys just got here, so here are some 'survival tips,'" she said as we all sat down for a drink in the campus cafeteria. "First of all, you should know that this is a country of soldiers. Many Israeli adults have spent some time in the army. You may have noticed from the way they drive here that their attitude is all about 'survival of the fittest.'"

I nodded, thinking back to the taxi ride in from the airport. The mere memory of it sent a wave of nausea through my belly. I took a long sip of my ginger ale. Thank God you could get Canada Dry here!

"You've also probably noticed by now that security is a way of life here," Sharon continued. "Be prepared to get searched when you enter the mall or other public places. And don't be shocked to see armed soldiers everywhere you go: restaurants, shops, buses."

The gingery bubbles melted on my tongue as I ate up her words. I knew that this was the kind of stuff I needed to hear if I was going to make a life for myself in this city — even if it was for just three months.

"Be respectful around the Orthodox Jews," Sharon continued. "You'll know them by the way they're dressed."

My thoughts flashed back to the men I'd seen walking through the airport. Big black hats, long dark coats. My dad and his cape were going to fit right in.

"And it's important to remember that these people don't believe in any eye contact or physical contact — even handshaking — between members of the opposite sex. In fact, Mackenzie, if you ever take a seat on a bus next to an Orthodox man, don't be surprised if he gets up and moves away. You should also know that much of this city shuts down from Friday afternoon until Saturday night at sunset. Whatever you do, don't drive through a religious neighbourhood during that time. You might have stones or even dirty diapers thrown at you."

"Oh *gross!*" I grimaced and put down my drink. "Are you serious?"

"One hundred per cent," Sharon replied with a laugh. "It's just a fact of life here. Don't worry, you'll get used to it soon enough."

No I won't, because I'm not going to be staying, I felt like replying.

When Dad got up to refill his coffee cup, Sharon leaned her head towards mine and lowered her voice to a whisper.

"Listen, I'm sure this whole thing hasn't been easy for you ... you know, moving to a strange country without your mother here to help. So if you don't mind, I'd like to offer you some 'woman-to-woman' advice."

I stared down at my drink and shrugged. As nice as Sharon seemed, I did *not* want to talk to her about Mom. *Please don't go there*, I prayed silently.

"Mackenzie, I want you to promise me that you'll be careful when you're out alone," Sharon continued. "You're in the Middle East, now — a long way from North America. There are people and places in this city that can be dangerous for young girls on their own. Do you understand?"

I looked up again and nodded, relieved that she hadn't asked about Mom. And happy that she didn't give me that speech in front of Dad. He was way too overprotective of me already without hearing stuff like that. Too bad he couldn't be more like Sharon. I liked how she spoke to me like an adult, without sugar-coating the facts to make this place seem more like home.

Still, there was no way I could have known just how accurate her warning would turn out to be.

Chapter 3

∿∿

On our fourth day in Jerusalem, Dad took me sight-seeing.

"Wake up and put on your walking shoes!" he said, opening my curtains to let in the bright morning light. "We're going to the Old City today!"

I opened my eyes and groaned. He was standing over my bed and smiling down at me in full tourist gear: Birkenstocks, safari hat, and Bermuda shorts. Ugh! At least he wasn't wearing his cape. Dad had been known around York University as a bit of an oddball — a reputation I know secretly pleased him. Every time I ever visited him at work, I'd find him riding an old-fashioned bicycle around campus, his black cape billowing behind him in the wind. He told me that his students had long ago nicknamed him Einstein because of his wild mop of bushy, blond hair. I sometimes called him that, too, but never to his face. Can't you just picture him? If he wasn't my father, I'd laugh. But most of the time I don't find him very funny.

Still, as much as I sometimes hate to admit it, Dad and I are eerily similar in a lot of ways. We both sleep with our eyes halfway open, we're both allergic to strawberries, and we both have the same dumb laugh that has politely been compared to a horse on drugs. We also have the same abnormally long pinkie toes, the same lopsided smiles, and the same pasty white skin — for sure my worst feature. Dad calls it "alabaster," but it's so grossly pale the kids at school back home nicknamed me Snow White. I could never get a nice suntan like the other girls and I couldn't even wear shorts in the summertime without looking like a ghost.

Which was exactly how Dad was looking right now in his Bermuda shorts. Weird how genetics work, huh?

But we have our differences as well, and that's usually what the fights are about. Maybe it's because he's an archaeologist, but his head always seems to be stuck in the past — the ancient past. So much so that he usually doesn't give a rat's ass about what's happening right in front of his nose. It's something that used to drive Mom crazy. And I worried it was only going to get worse here in Israel.

Still, I had to admit, as much as I didn't want to come here, the old walled city of Jerusalem turned out to be a pretty interesting place. It was made up of four quarters, one each for the Christians, Jews, Muslims, and Armenians. Cars weren't allowed on the Old City streets. Each quarter was a maze of narrow cobbled roads, staircases, sharp angles, dark passages, and tiny corners that demanded to be explored on foot.

Instead of taking a formal tour, Dad suggested that we just wander around on our own.

"It's more exciting this way," he said, his grey-blue eyes gleaming. "Who knows? Maybe we'll even get lost!"

It didn't take very long to see how easily that could happen. With crowds of people walking in every direction, twisting roads, and a jumble of haphazard old buildings, arches, and domes, the Old City oozed a sense of exotic chaos. Unlike Toronto, where the streets followed a well-planned grid, there was absolutely nothing orderly about this place.

We started off in the bustling Muslim quarter. With all the ancient buildings and sites, Dad was totally in his element. For the first time in my life, I got an idea of why he was so popular with his students: he really had a way of making history come alive.

"This is the Damascus Gate, which was originally built by the Romans," he explained. "And over here is the Via Dolorosa, the path where it's believed Jesus walked carrying his cross. And down this way is the Dome of the Rock, a mosque that dates back to the seventh century. It's one of the most important sites in all of Islam."

Normally, I wasn't too interested in religious buildings, but this one took my breath away. I had seen it before in photographs of Jerusalem, resting on top of the city like a gleaming crown. But up close, it was so much more magnificent. Covered in intricate blue, gold, and white mosaics, it was topped off with a gigantic golden dome that shone brilliantly in the bright Israeli sunlight.

It was a pretty hot morning, and the heat intensified as the day went on. Every minute the sun rose higher in the sky, I could feel it burning deeper and deeper into my skin. I tried to tell myself that heat was better than cold and I was lucky to be missing the Canadian winter this year. But in this kind of heat, even the thought of snow and sleet and slush was refreshing. As we walked, I drank a lot of water and tried to think cool thoughts.

Polar bears ... tobogganing ... ice fishing ... snowball fights ... wind chill factors ...

It didn't help much.

After wandering around for a while, we suddenly found ourselves in the Arab market, or "souk," as it was called here. We paused at the entrance and watched the hustle and bustle for a few minutes. The crowds were thick with all kinds of people: American tourists in their baseball caps and fanny packs, women covered in scarves, and men with heads draped in black-and-white checkered fabric.

I closed my eyes and took in a deep breath of the exotic market air. It was absolutely bursting with smells: spices, coffee, smoke, ripe fruit, and vegetables. I opened my eyes again and stared down the long, sloping path of the market. It was lined with hundreds of vendors balancing on rickety chairs outside their shops. Some of them were so ancient-looking their faces seemed like they'd been sculpted out of rubber. I knew it wasn't polite, but I just couldn't stop staring at them. They looked as old as the city itself — like they'd been sitting there on those chairs since the beginning of time. And they were selling just about every kind of merchandise imaginable: copper, gold, and silver jewellery; ceramics; fabric; clothes; shoes;

pastries; produce; spices; and every souvenir under the sun.

Their cries were piercing as we strolled by their stores.

"Hallo, Hallo!"

"Come take a look!"

"Please, please — you want souvenirs?"

"Right here, best prices in Jerusalem!"

"Hey, it's past lunchtime. Do you want to try a falafel?" Dad asked, pointing to a nearby stand. "It's, like, the national dish here."

I walked over to take a closer look. Just like on the first day we arrived, an overwhelming aroma of spice and frying oil wafted under my nose. A skinny, dark man with a chipped front tooth was putting brown, deep-fried balls of mashed-up chickpeas into a pita pocket and covering the whole thing with sauce and vegetables. Of course, I'd *seen* falafels back in Toronto ... but I'd never actually eaten one before.

"C'mon," Dad said, pulling out his wallet. "I'll have one if you will."

"Um, okay."

I was getting hungry, and Dad's sense of adventure was contagious.

"Where are you from?" asked the skinny man as he stuffed my pita full to bulging. "Let me guess: England? Australia?"

"No," I replied timidly. Nobody had ever asked me that question before. "We're from Canada."

"Ahhhh!" he nodded. "My cousin lives in Canada. He says it's very cold there."

"Yeah, sometimes," I laughed, wiping the sweat off my forehead with the back of my hand. I felt like saying, *Dude, anywhere in the world would probably seem cold compared to this place!*

"There you go — enjoy!" he grinned, handing me his stuffed creation.

With a polite "thank you," I took a small bite and chewed it cautiously, waiting for my taste buds to make a decision. The falafel was crunchy, hot, spicy ... and surprisingly tasty.

"It's good!" I proclaimed, taking another bite. Dad beamed with pleasure, like the falafel somehow justified this whole move to the Middle East.

We finished our lunch and took our time strolling, browsing, and taking in all the incredible sights of the market. After poking around for a couple of hours, we ended up on a stone terrace overlooking the Western Wall — an ancient, open-air synagogue where tons of people had gathered to pray.

"This is the holiest site in the Jewish religion," Dad explained as we gazed down on the crowd. "This one wall is all that remains of the ancient Temple of Jerusalem. It's been standing for more than two thousand years."

Standing a fair distance back, I strained my eyes and tried to see what all the fuss was about. The Wall looked old, fragile, proud.

"Maybe we can go and take a closer look," I suggested.

But Dad shook his head and pointed down to our shorts and tank tops. "Not today. You have to be covered up to go near the Wall. Next time, we'll bring better clothes."

I nodded silently as my thoughts flicked back to that return ticket.

No, Dad. There's not going to be a next time.

On the fifth day, I was on my own while Dad went to meet some colleagues at the university. It was time to start exploring the neighbourhood. With Professor Anderson's advice still fresh in my head, I was a bit apprehensive about leaving the apartment by myself. But in the end, I was more restless than nervous. I figured it would probably be safe enough to check out the local sights.

A few doors down from our building, I stumbled upon a little corner store that was like no other corner store I'd ever seen before in my life. There was no sign outside — no storefront name — just a door and a big cigarette advertisement marking the spot. I stepped inside to look around.

"Oh, wow!" I gasped under my breath. The entire store was just a tiny little hole in the wall, jam-packed with shelves that stretched from floor to ceiling. The shelves were stuffed with things like toilet paper, bags of chips, bottles of pop and water, cleaning products, and cigarettes.

A dark-skinned boy about my age stood behind a narrow counter laden with sweet rolls and candy. Even from a distance, I noticed his eyes. They were gorgeous — big and round, and the exact colour of café-au-lait. Although he looked tall, I still couldn't help wondering how he was able to reach up to the top row of shelves that grazed the ceiling of his store.

Noticing me noticing him, the boy nodded and smiled at me. I smiled shyly back. I wanted to say hello, but didn't know how.

Smart move, Mack-on-Crack! Next time maybe you'll look up some Hebrew phrases before walking out the door!

And since I hadn't brought any money along, I couldn't buy anything from him. Feeling stupid and not knowing what else to do, I left the store to continue exploring.

A few steps further down the street, I came across the busy intersection I'd seen from my window. Traffic was flying past at a frightening pace and a never-ending symphony of horns filled the air. I stood a safe distance back from the curb and watched the commotion of cars with horror and awe. For the first time in my teenage life, I was actually grateful that I was too young for a driver's licence.

Suddenly, a low mumbling caught my attention. I turned and saw a young, bearded man standing next to me, bowing his head and reciting some strange-sounding words. I listened carefully, but couldn't make out what he was saying — I could only assume it was Hebrew. I knew I shouldn't be staring, but it was hard not to. I'd never seen anybody pray in a public place before and it left me with a funny feeling — curious and uncomfortable at the same time. It seemed so personal, like he'd decided to take off his clothes right beside me.

Crossing the street, I watched the hustle and bustle of the intersection for a while. When the heat and the dust became too much to handle, I turned to head back to the safety of the apartment. Coming in from the heat was a welcome relief. I kicked off my sweaty sandals, enjoying the feel of the chilly tiles on my hot feet.

Peeling off the rest of my clothes, I jumped straight into a cool shower to wash off the coating of dust that was clinging to my body. It seemed like everything in this country was covered in a layer of powdery archaeology.

I guess it was finally making a bit of sense why Dad wanted to come and work here so badly.

On the sixth day, I met Marla.

I decided to venture out a little bit further and bring along some money, although truthfully, I didn't know how to count it or how much I had. I walked past the busy intersection until I came to a series of stores. There was a pizzeria, a flower shop, a movie-rental store, a café, a falafel stand, and a tiny accessory store, all getting ready to open up for business.

I stood back and watched as awnings were un-rolled, stoops were swept, and patio chairs were set up.

Even though it was still early in the morning, the heat was getting intense. Already, beads of sweat were beginning to dot my upper lip and trickle down my neck. Looking for something to cool me down, I wandered into the pizza joint and spied a large freezer filled with ice cream and popsicles.

Yes!

I ran over, opened up the door, and basked in the surge of cold, manufactured air that rushed out into my face. After a minute, I chose an ice cream bar that, from the photo on the package, looked like a wedge of pink watermelon.

"I'd like to buy this, please," I said timidly, not sure whether the cashier spoke English or not. I grabbed a handful of coins from my pocket and held them out hopefully. Smiling, she gently plucked the correct amount out of my palm.

"Tank yoo," she said in a heavily accented voice. I smiled back and turned to go. I couldn't help feeling proud of myself for accomplishing this smallest of tasks. I know, it's silly, right? But it was a hot day in the Middle East and I'd bought myself an ice cream! Maybe I'd be able to get along here, after all.

But everything changed a second later when I peeled open the wrapper and my triumph instantly crumbled to pieces onto the floor. Flustered, I turned back to the cashier and pointed to the rapidly melting mess of pink and green.

"I just opened it," I tried to explain. "The ice cream was already broken — it's not my fault."

But apparently, her knowledge of English stopped at "thank you." Suddenly, her smile disappeared and she started gesturing wildly with her hands.

"*K-hee ohd. K-hee ohd,*" she insisted loudly.

With my face turning red from embarrassment and my feet frozen to the floor, all I could do was just shake my head like an idiot to let her know I didn't understand. But with every second that passed, she just got louder and more boisterous.

"*K-hee ohd. K-hee ohd — k-hee ohd achad!*" she repeated, almost yelling now as she gestured towards the mess.

"What? What?"

I had no idea what she was saying. Was she calling me clumsy? Did she want me to clean it up? Was she kicking me out of her pizzeria? Just as I was about to run out the door, a voice from behind came to my rescue.

"Don't worry," the voice explained in perfect North American English. "She's just trying to tell you to take another one."

I spun around and came face to face with a girl exactly my own height. She had a mane of brown curls, a high regal forehead, a nose full of freckles, and yellowy-green eyes that were almost the exact colour of the raw olives growing in the tree outside my apartment.

"She sounds angry, but she's really not," the girl continued. "She's just Israeli — they're very passionate here."

"Oh — well, thanks," I stammered. "I, um, don't speak any Hebrew."

"Yeah, I kind of figured that one out. So, are you a tourist?"

"Not exactly," I replied, reaching into the freezer for another ice cream bar, much to the obvious relief of the cashier. "I just moved to Jerusalem this week. My name's Mackenzie. Mackenzie Hill."

"Nice to meet you. I'm Marla Hoffman. Hey, we've got the same initials."

Outside the pizzeria, we fell in step and continued our conversation. I licked my ice cream happily; I had no idea where we were going, nor did I really care. It was just nice to talk to somebody in English.

It turned out that Marla was sixteen, had moved here from Buffalo, New York five years ago, and lived in an apartment building just down the street from ours.

"I speak Hebrew and I know my way around. So if you want, I can show you the city in the afternoons when I get off work," she offered.

I eagerly accepted. By the time my ice cream was finished, we'd forged the beginnings of a new friendship.

And what did I do on the seventh day? Simple. I took it easy and chillaxed — just like they did in the Bible — and, for the first time since we landed, thought about all the possibilities this new world had to offer.

Chapter 4

~~~

Marla was fantastic! Like, the coolest person I'd ever known. I felt giddy when we were together, like I'd fallen head over heels in love with a new best friend (in a totally hetero way, of course).

She was funny, daring, independent, worldly, outspoken. She knew how to drive, spoke three languages, and didn't care what anybody said about her. She had streaks in her hair, a pierced belly button, and no curfew. Unlike my dad, *her* father sounded great. He let her drink wine with dinner. And he let her date. She'd had two boyfriends in the past year and was more than happy to share the wisdom of her experience with me.

But the best thing of all about Marla was that she didn't feel sorry for me. For the first time in over a year I wasn't "tragic." And that felt good.

Unfortunately, I was so excited to have a new friend that I forgot one of the cardinal rules of being a teenager: *Never* reveal too much to a parent — especially one as overprotective and unpredictable as my dad.

When I told him the story of how Marla and I met, the first thing he did was sign me up for an intensive course in Hebrew.

"You need to be able to get around this city," he said. "We can't have another incident like that one in the pizzeria."

"But Dad," I protested, "Marla knows Hebrew. She can translate for me."

"Sorry honey, but you have to learn it for yourself. And you'll need it when you start school in the fall — many of your classes will be in Hebrew."

I stared at him in shock.

"But ... but Dad, I'm only going to be here for three months. It'll just be a waste of money."

He laughed at that. "Let me worry about the money, Mack."

"And what about you?" I challenged. "You don't know any Hebrew. Are you going to take a class, too?"

"Me? Gosh no. I'm far too busy planning my curriculum for the fall semester. Tell you what, you can teach me what you learn every day. It'll be fun."

Yeah, really fun — like watching weeds grow!

As much as I tried to talk him out of it, no amount of whining, begging, or complaining seemed to help. His mind was made up.

So that's how I ended up in school for the last seven weeks of summer. Me and my stupid big mouth!

Marla tried to reassure me that it wasn't going to be so bad.

"Everyone who comes to Israel takes language classes — it's almost like an initiation rite. My family and I all did it together. It's called 'Ulpan.'"

But she was wrong. It was *so* bad. The classroom was hot, the teacher made the class more boring than last-period geometry, and all my classmates reeked of cigarettes. Thankfully, I only had to be there in the mornings. I spent much of my time in Ulpan doodling, staring out the window, and wondering where we were going to spend our afternoon.

Marla had a summer job at a nearby day camp. Since her work ended at twelve-thirty, she was able to meet me every day after class to take me around the city — just like she'd promised.

The first thing she did was teach me how to navigate the Israeli bus system. Then she showed me the sights. She took me to downtown Jerusalem to see all the great shops and chic boutiques. She took me to the bustling Yoel Solomon Street to window-shop at all the trendy stores. She took me to Mahane Yehuda, the huge open-air food market, where we browsed and munched on free tastes of everything from sunflower seeds and homemade candy to baked goods and freshly churned peanut butter. She took me to Emek Refaim, a pretty neighbourhood packed with cafés and restaurants. She took me to Liberty Bell Park and showed me the Terry Fox Garden, which made my heart swell with pride for Canada and my stomach queasy with homesickness all at the same time. She pointed out all the posh, swanky hotels where royalty, ambassadors, and heads of state came to stay on their official visits to Jerusalem.

And then the next day she taught me how to sneak into the posh, swanky hotel pools.

"All you need is one of these to look like you belong," she explained, pulling a pair of towels out of her beach bag.

I took one and examined it. It was thick and fluffy and soft. And embroidered in fancy print were the words, *The King David Hotel.*

"Where did you get this?" I asked.

"I've got a whole bunch of them at home," she

explained. "My grandmother is rich, but cheap. Nothing gives her more pleasure in life than to get stuff for free. She stashes hotel towels in her suitcase every time she visits from Buffalo. I have towels from all the nicest hotels in Jerusalem."

I couldn't believe she was bragging about this!

"So, your grandmother's a kleptomaniac?" I asked, handing her back the stolen towel before anybody saw me holding it. She just laughed and stuffed it back into her bag.

"Don't be so paranoid, Mack!"

Paranoid or not, the first time we snuck into a hotel pool I felt like a criminal.

"What if we get caught?" I moaned. My heart was beating a mile a minute. I'd never done anything so reckless before.

"We won't," Marla said, pulling me towards the lounge chairs. "Just act like you belong. And pay with shekels for anything you buy."

I was so nervous. I chose a chair as far away from the pool as possible, pulled the brim of my hat down over my face, and started nibbling my fingernails furiously. I fully expected the police to show up and haul us off to jail. My skin was itchy under my bikini. I tugged awkwardly at the straps, and prayed we wouldn't get caught.

Marla, on the other hand, seemed totally relaxed. She stretched out her towel, pulled out her iPod, and started sunbathing. I have to admit, after an hour I began to ease up a bit. I even took off my hat and let my face show. And at the end of the day, when I realized that nobody was going to arrest me for trespassing, I was hooked. After that, it got easier and easier every time.

In between the sights and the pools, Marla taught me how to "coffee." Coffee, you see, is a whole cultural movement in Israel. Espresso bars and outdoor cafés are everywhere. In the early afternoon, everything slows down for a couple of hours while people flock to the coffee shops to relax and escape the heat.

Marla almost fell off her chair when I told her I'd never tasted coffee before.

"What are you talking about? Not even a sip? Are you from this planet?"

"I guess I never thought much about it." I shrugged. My mind skipped back a couple of months to Hailey Winthrop and her story of her date with Harrison Finch. We'd all been so shocked when she'd tasted his coffee.

"Doesn't caffeine stunt your growth?" I asked Marla.

"Um, are you planning on a career in professional basketball?"

"No," I muttered stupidly.

Marla sighed and pushed her steaming cup into my hands. "Look, Mack, I used to be an outsider in this country too, so here's some advice. You don't smoke and that's okay. But if you don't learn to like coffee, you'll *never* fit in. So drink up!"

I took a tentative sip and grimaced. It was black, burning hot, and bitter.

"Ugh! You like this stuff?" I asked, handing her back the cup.

Marla giggled. "I do, but I've had a lot of practice. Maybe I should have started you off with something a bit easier."

She got me another cup and sweetened it with milk and sugar until it tasted like a hot dessert. Better, but still not as satisfying as a hot chocolate on a wintry afternoon. Despite my protests, Marla kept dragging me back into coffee shops every day.

"It's for your own good!" she'd insist, pushing cup after cup into my hands.

Wouldn't you know it? By the time August was over, I was drinking it like a pro. I was also getting around the city like a pro and even speaking the language. I guess the Ulpan was doing its job.

So there I was, a million miles away from my old life in Canada. I'd gone from a nervous tourist to being almost as street savvy as a native Jerusalemite. I'd developed a caffeine habit and spent my mornings learning Hebrew and my afternoons floating on an air mattress in the King David Hotel pool, rubbing elbows with princes and prime ministers.

Oh my God — it was turning into the best summer of my entire life!

Chapter 5

~~~

She was coming into the store almost every day now and, even though Nasir knew it was wrong, he couldn't take his eyes off her. Her skin was so pale, it seemed to be almost transparent. And with her long yellow hair and blue eyes, he thought she looked just like the American doll that his sister Amar kept hidden under her bed — away from the disapproving eyes of their parents.

He wanted to say something to her. He wanted to say, *Hi, my name is Nasir ... what's yours?* He was so sure that's what they would say in America. He was sure that's where she came from.

Every time she came to the store, he would watch her wandering up and down the aisles pretending to shop. He knew she was pretending because all she ever bought was gum and candy. He thought she looked timid and lost — like she didn't know how she arrived or where she was going next. Lately, he spent most of his free time at work daydreaming about her beautiful face and staring out the grimy store window, waiting for her to come back.

His keys jangled in his jeans pocket with each step he took towards home. With no customers in the last hour, he'd decided to close up the store a few minutes early. He knew his boss wouldn't mind — it's not as if business had been booming. In fact, lately their best customer had been the "gum girl."

As he neared his home, he shook his head to clear his mind of her, worried that his thoughts would some-how shine through his eyes and betray him to his parents. The sun was starting to go down behind the Old City walls as he entered the building and climbed the stairs to his family's apartment. As soon as he opened the door, a familiar smell filled his nose. His stomach growled with hunger: he knew right away Mama was cooking baed u batata, his favourite dish. Heading straight for the kitchen, he kissed his mother and leaned down to greet his sisters. Sameera and Amar were help-ing with dinner while Rana crawled underfoot, mop-ping the floor with her favourite rag doll. Hearing his son arrive, Mr. Hadad hurried over to say hello.

"Nasir! How was your work today?" he cried, kissing his cheeks three times.

"It was fine, Baba," he replied, returning his father's embrace. His father was quite tall, but so was Nasir. Not long ago, Nasir would have to stand on his toes to reach his father, but in the last year he'd grown so fast that he now matched his height.

"You're just in time for dinner," Baba said, leading Nasir over to the tiny dining table. "Come sit down and tell me what happened."

While father and son sat and discussed the details of their day, Mama and the two older girls brought the dishes to the table. They started the meal with mezze: olives, hummus, baba ganoush, and tabouleh. Sameera passed around freshly baked loaves of taboon bread, which they tore into small pieces to scoop up the dips. They continued with the baed u batata — cubed potatoes and eggs fried in olive oil and allspice — and ended with fruit and mint tea.

Throughout the meal, Mama pressed them all to refill their plates several times — she was only ever truly happy when those dining at her table had stuffed themselves. As usual, she served herself only after everyone else had finished.

When the meal was over, the family sat back in their

chairs and lingered over their empty plates and full stomachs. Sameera told a story about two of her girlfriends from school, giggling and covering her mouth so much that her words were almost unintelligible. In contrast to Sameera, Nasir's middle sister, Amar, was quite shy. Her parents tried to persuade her to perform the little song she was learning in her class, but she blushed and ran to Mama's lap, burying her face in the folds of her dress. Baby Rana, who was still learning how to feed herself, sat in Mama's arms, babbling and fingerpainting her round cheeks with the leftover hummus. As messy as she was, her older siblings couldn't help kissing her.

By the time the table was cleared, it was getting late. One by one, Mama began carrying the sleepy girls to their bed. Once they were alone, Mr. Hadad pulled Nasir aside to talk.

"There's something I'd like to speak to you about," he said, motioning for his son to join him on the couch — the same couch that would be Nasir's bed in just a few more hours. Nasir sat down beside him, guessing from the low hang of his father's eyebrows that this was going to be serious. He was right.

"I don't know if you've overheard Mama and me talking about it, but our family in Askar is in real trouble. Your grandparents' health is not good, and your aunt has just lost her job. They need our help. We have to start sending more money."

Nasir nodded. He knew that their relatives in the West Bank had a terrible life. Compared to the way they lived over there, their own tiny apartment in Jerusalem was luxurious. Ever since Nasir could remember, his parents had been sending money to support them.

"I know you've been helping out with your salary from the store," he continued. "But it's just not enough."

Nasir nodded again. "What do you want me to do?"

Baba leaned his head close to his son's and lowered his voice to a barely audible whisper. Clearly, he didn't want Mama to hear what he was about to say. But that would be difficult. Their apartment was too small to keep many secrets — a fact that was made embarrassingly clear to Nasir every few nights when noises from his parents' room travelled through the walls and into his mortified ears.

"I've found a way to make some extra money," he whispered. "I'm going to need your help and strong arms to do it. It's going to mean hard work and late hours — you might have to miss some soccer games."

Nasir watched his father's eyes moisten with sadness as he spoke. Baba had grown up in Askar, moving to Jerusalem only after his parents arranged his marriage to Mama, who was already an Israeli citizen. Because of the tight border regulations, he'd only been back to visit them a handful of times over the past twenty years. Nasir could only guess how hard it was for him to be away from his family. And it was probably even harder not to have enough money to support them.

Years ago, Baba used to earn a decent living as a tour guide. But ever since the second intifada began, the whole tourism industry had really suffered. Lately he'd only been working sporadically. As the oldest child and only son, Nasir had always known that he would one day be expected to stand beside his father and help support their family. But he never imagined the day would come when he would be asked to take a *second* job. And especially not while he was only sixteen.

The call to prayer sounded in the distance, bringing a quick end to their conversation. Baba jumped up from the couch and reached for his prayer rug, which had been carefully rolled and placed in the corner of the room. Nasir went to get his, too. The Hadad household was a fairly traditional one. Mama still covered her hair in public and Baba prayed five times every day. He expected his son to pray, too, and Nasir went along with it to please him. Over the years, this had all become a well-established routine.

In almost perfect synchrony they washed their hands, removed their shoes, turned towards Mecca, and rolled out their prayer rugs side by side on the floor. Then they dropped to their knees and brought their foreheads down to meet the matted woollen fibres of their rugs.

But that is where the similarities of their routines ended. As usual, while Baba started praying, Nasir's mind began to wander. Against all his best efforts, his thoughts crept back to the girl. He wondered if she'd ever noticed him watching her. He wondered what it must be like to have the money to waste on gum and candy every day. He wondered what her name was and what her voice sounded like.

Every time she came up to the counter he opened his mouth to talk to her, but always ended up losing his courage. Maybe he would manage to say something tomorrow — he was almost certain she'd be back.

Turning his head slightly, he snuck a quick peek at his father praying so intently beside him. Their conversation replayed itself again in his mind. He knew his father felt guilty for living in Israel while their relatives languished in a refugee camp. Nasir sometimes wondered whether he should feel guilty, too. But he never did. He was very happy not to be over there. In fact, most of the time he didn't even want to be over *here*. He couldn't imagine living the rest of his life this way. There were places in the world where people didn't have to struggle so hard to support their families — places in the world where life was easier. Nasir knew this for a fact.

Just then, Baba opened his eyes and saw his son watching him. Nasir quickly turned his eyes back down to his rug and continued on through the motions of his prayer.

Chapter 6

~~~

I decided the dark-skinned boy with the big brown eyes had a crush on me.

Although we hadn't spoken yet, I was almost positive it was true. Every time I went into in his little hole-in-the-wall store, his eyes would follow me up and down the aisles. Even when he was helping another customer, it seemed like he was always watching me. It was pretty shameless — he didn't even try to hide it. And I could see his hands trembling whenever I came up to the counter.

It made me nervous. I didn't know what to say; I didn't know what to do, either. It was just so embarrassing.

Sometimes I'd steal a glance or two from underneath the thin veil of my hair while he was busy at the cash register. He had thick dark hair that was almost long enough to brush his shoulders, smooth tanned skin, and a thin white scar cutting across the bottom of his chin.

And of course, those eyes! They were rimmed with lashes so long and dark that he almost looked like he was wearing mascara. Every time I looked at him I felt jealous. Why should a boy have lashes like that? My own blond eyelashes were practically invisible.

At first I only dropped into the store on my way to Ulpan when I needed something like a pack of gum or a roll of Life Savers. Every time I walked in I could feel the intensity of his gaze. Those brown eyes would burn into me until I had no choice but to just get out of there as fast as I could. But I would always find myself coming back for more a few days later. I have to admit, it was flattering. Never in my life had a boy stared at me like that, and I'd begun to like it. I couldn't put my finger on it, but there was something unusual about him — something different from the guys I went to school with back in Canada. I started finding excuses to go to his store as often as I could. I must have seemed like a crazy girl with an obsessive gum habit, but it was the only thing I could afford to buy on such a regular basis. I wondered what he thought of me and why he looked at me that way. Harrison Finch never once looked at Hailey Wintrop like that, and they'd almost gone all the way!

When I told Marla about it, her reaction surprised me.

"You mean that Arab boy at the local *makolet*?" she gasped.

"Mako-what?"

"Trust me, you've got to forget about him!" she warned, ignoring my question. "Sure he's cute, but he's also Muslim! His parents will never let him date you!"

"I never said I wanted to date him!" I replied, suddenly feeling very defensive. "I just think he's nice looking. And anyway, why not?"

"Why not? Don't you see?" she asked, shaking her finger at me. "You're white and Christian. It's *not* going to happen!"

Still, I couldn't get him out of my head. I dreamed about him at night. I got dressed in the mornings totally based on what I thought he'd like. It's funny, at home just bumping into a guy wouldn't put me over the edge like this, but I guess when you're in a foreign country, any male attention is better than nothing. Soon enough, I found myself going into his shop every single day. Between coffee and gum, I was running out of money fast.

I think I was getting a crush on him, too. And I didn't even know his name!

Chapter 7

〜〜〜

By coincidence, my fifteenth birthday fell on the last day of Ulpan.

I don't know if Dad called and told him or what, but somehow my teacher got wind of it and led the whole class in a shaky chorus of the Hebrew happy birthday song. As you can imagine, it was mortifying. Of course, I turned red as a beet. I always do when people sing "Happy Birthday" to me.

Later that night, Dad took me out for dinner at a local shish kebab place and gave me my present over a plate of shwarma. At first when I opened the box and found a cellphone, I was ecstatic. Pretty awesome birthday present, right? Well, as it turned out, not so much.

"This is for emergency use only, Mack," Dad explained in his most authoritative parental tone. "I get nervous with you running all over this city and I want you to be safe. But you'll have no more than ten minutes of call time per month, so use it wisely."

Um, hello? What was I supposed to do with ten minutes a month? For a teenager, it was like getting a key to the candy store and being told you could only have one jelly bean. Not wanting to hurt his feelings, I smiled and did my best to hide my disappointment. After all, what did I expect? Mom had always been the one to buy the presents in our family — Dad would just sign the card and show up for cake.

Presents aside, now that I was fifteen, what I had *really* been hoping for was the green light to start dating. When I brought it up, though, Dad looked pained — like someone had just stuck a pin in his butt.

"Well, uh — I don't think this is the right time to discuss that, Mack," he stammered.

My heart sunk. This was not how I'd imagined this conversation happening. At this rate, I was *never* going to have a boyfriend!

"What do you mean 'not the right time'?" I whined, trying to keep from crying. "I'm *fifteen years old* now, Dad. *All* my friends are dating!"

That last part wasn't exactly true, but I thought it made my argument sound more convincing. Unfortunately, Dad didn't agree.

"Oh gosh," he said, pushing his couscous nervously around with his fork, "Let's wait a little bit longer on this one, okay, honey?"

I could hear a slight hint of begging in his voice; I knew he was dying to drop the subject, and it didn't take a genius to figure out why. In all his years as a parent, he'd never imagined having this conversation with me. Mom had always handled the tough parenting subjects. You know, the birds-and-bees talk, the first-period talk, the say-no-to-drugs talk. He'd been on the sidelines of my childhood, and probably never expected he'd have to handle the ready-to-start-dating talk all by himself!

Maybe it was because it was my birthday, but I was feeling kind of generous. So, in a rare moment of weakness, I took pity on him and let him off the hook — for now, anyway.

After my birthday I began to see less of him as he started working longer hours at the university getting ready for the beginning of the first semester. Sometimes he wouldn't get home until after dark. Of course, I was always there waiting for him. The local pizza guy already knew our order by heart.

Some things never change.

At least Ulpan was finally over. And there were still a couple of weeks before the beginning of school in

October, so Marla suggested we celebrate the end of summer by going on a trip to a nearby beach town called Netanya.

Naturally, Dad didn't want to let me go, but when I promised to be home for dinner he finally agreed. We hopped on a bus early in the morning and got there just over an hour later. Unlike Canada, where it would take weeks to get from one end of the country to the other, nothing in Israel is very far. They say the entire nation is about the size of New Jersey.

The first things I noticed in Netanya were the palm trees. They were everywhere, as abundant as maple trees back at home. And there were miles of the most beautiful sandy beaches I'd ever seen. We spent the whole time splashing in the Mediterranean, eating ice cream, and lounging on the sand — Marla in the sunshine working on her tan and me right next to her, under an umbrella, slathered with SPF 45.

While we lay there, I thought a bit about my friends back home and how they'd spent their summer sitting on the banks of the mud-bottom lake at Camp Towango. Steffi would have been so jealous of this beach. Scratch that — *all* my old friends would have been jealous if they could see where I was. God, it's amazing how quickly you can lose touch with people.

I'd barely spoken or written to any of them all summer. And you know what? I wasn't missing them at all. Not even Christina. It was strange to think that in only a couple of weeks I'd be seeing them again when I flew back home to Toronto.

I dreamt about the beach that night — the blue water, the soft sand, the warm breeze, and the cloudless sky. When I woke up the next morning it was almost eleven o'clock. I stretched my arms lazily up in the air, enjoying the feel of a good sleep-in. But just as I was getting out of bed, a deafening noise pierced the air.

"Waaaaaa-oooooo ... waaaaaaa-ooooooooo ... waaaaaaa-ooooooooo ... waaaaaaa-ooooooooo ..."

I almost jumped out of my skin.

Oh my God! The air raid siren!

My brain seized up with fear as I tried to remember what to do.

Are we under attack? Are bombs falling on us?

Panicked, I grabbed Frou-frou and Mom's sweater (her picture still inside) and ran to the bomb shelter. My heart was pounding out of my chest. The siren was so loud, so constant, and so urgent. There was no escaping it.

I can't believe I'm all alone! Daddy! Daddy! I wish you were here with me!

I grabbed a gas mask and pulled it over my face, then set to work sealing the doors with duct tape. The siren screamed in my ears the whole time.

"Waaaaaa-oooooo ... waaaaaaa-oooooooooo ... waaaaaaa-ooooooooo ... waaaaaaa-oooooooooo ..."

Oh no! Somebody help me! I don't want to die! What do I do now? Where's the instruction sheet?

I found it and frantically began reading the directions.

<u>In Case of Emergency</u>
Bring radio into shelter.

Damn it! I messed up the very first instruction!

I stared at the sealed door and imagined a giant green cloud of poisonous gas forming on the other side.

Oh well ... too late to go get the radio now!

I sat down on the floor and started to cry. I felt more hideously alone in that moment than ever before in my entire life. A couple of terrifying minutes later, the siren stopped just as abruptly as it had started. What did that mean? I wiped my eyes under the gas mask and checked the instruction sheet. My breath sounded like Darth Vader.

Do <u>not</u> leave until you hear the
"all-clear" signal.

I cowered in the corner and waited. I had no idea what an all-clear signal was supposed to sound like, but I figured I'd know it when I heard it.

Hours went by; the morning passed into afternoon. I was sure we were at war. I strained my ears to listen for gunfire, but I couldn't hear anything besides my own breathing in the stupid gas mask. My face was hot and sweaty and uncomfortable, but I was too scared of the poisonous gas to take it off. I thought about Dad and prayed that he was all right and that he'd made it to the university bomb shelter. And for the first time ever, I found myself wishing I hadn't been so hard on him all this time. After all, he was hurting, too.

Feeling desperately alone, I picked up Mom's sweater and pulled the neck down carefully over my gas-masked head. At some point I must have fallen asleep, because the next thing I knew there was a loud *knock-knock* at the shelter door.

"Who's there?" I yelled, my whole body quivering with relief. Was it the army coming to save me?

"It's me, stupid," came a familiar voice from the other side. "What are you doing in there?"

"*Marla?*"

I jumped to my feet, un-duct-taped the door, and flung it open. "What do you mean 'what am *I* doing in here'?" I gasped. "What are *you* doing out *there*? Didn't you hear the air-raid siren?"

She started to laugh. "Um, *yeah*. But that was hours ago. Don't you have a radio? What were you waiting for, the army to personally come and release you?"

"No!" I lied. But I could see in her eyes that she knew she was right. My cheeks burned red with embarrassment. Thank God for the gas mask. I kept it on for a little longer to give my face a chance to turn back to its regular colour. "So, how'd you find me in here?"

"We were supposed to meet for coffee today, re-member? I waited and waited, but when you didn't come, I figured something might be wrong. I knew this was your building, so I came to find you and see if you were all right. By the way, you shouldn't leave your door unlocked. That might be okay in Canada, but not here."

"Yeah, okay. So, were we bombed? Or gassed? Are we at war?"

"No, lame-o. Next time listen to your radio! It was just a practice. They do that every now and then to keep us on our toes."

A practice? All that for a practice? I wasted a whole day in this prison for nothing? What kind of a stupid country is this?

Suddenly, I was mad. What a fool I was, waiting around with my teddy bear to be rescued! I ripped the gas mask off, threw it on the floor, and stomped out of the shelter. The look of amusement quickly disappeared from Marla's face.

"You know, everyone gets freaked out the first time they hear the siren," she said, following me to my room. "The first time I heard it go off was a couple of months after we got here from Buffalo. My poor cat actually jumped out the window! *Splat!*"

I didn't know if she was joking or not, but it didn't really matter, anyway. I was too pissed off to laugh.

"Cool apartment, Mack," she said, flopping down on my bed while I rummaged around in the closet for a pair of shorts. "Is your dad at work?"

"Yeah," I said, pulling them on. "Maybe you can meet him next time."

"Sure, whatever. So, where's your mom? Does she work at the university too?"

I froze in my tracks.

Oh my God! How am I going to tell her about Mom?

I turned around slowly and stared at her.

"Um, well ... you see ... um ..."

Make up a story, Mack!

"... my mom's ... um ..."

Say she's on a vacation ... or out grocery shopping or something!

"... she's, well ..."

Just say anything! You don't need her pity.

"... she's ... she's dead."

And there it was. The terrible awful truth, hanging in the air like a bad smell.

Suddenly serious, Marla sat upright on the bed. "I'm so sorry. What happened?"

I took a deep breath and let it out slowly. Back home the news had been splashed all over the TV and the papers. Everyone I knew had seen or read about it, which was good in a weird way because it had saved me from having to tell the story myself ... until now. For a split second I thought about making up a total lie, something less violent. But Marla was a good friend. I knew I owed her the truth.

I took another deep breath and closed my eyes.

"It was a hit and run. It happened down the street

from my house in Toronto. She was walking home from work. The driver ran a stop sign ... they never caught him. Her name was Elizabeth."

As simple as that. The facts of Mom's tragedy in fifty words or less. For Marla's sake, I left out all the truly horrible parts.

Like the blood-stained road. And how even after they scrubbed it clean and even after countless rainfalls, I could still see a shadow permanently ingrained in the pavement. And how I had to walk past it every morning on my way to school and every afternoon on my way home.

And I didn't mention how Mom's personal items were returned to us in a manila envelope: her watch, her wedding ring, her key chain, and her wallet, which I knew without even opening was still stuffed with my baby pictures.

And I didn't say anything about how my own twisted brain sometimes forced me to imagine her last, horrifying moments, seeing the car coming, freezing with fear, and knowing that she was about to die. And how often I tortured myself wondering if, in that split second, she thought about me.

I took the hem of Mom's sweater between my fingers and held it out for Marla to see.

"This was hers," I said as my thoughts flew back to the day I'd snuck into her closet to take it. It was right after Dad had told me about the move. Thinking about it now, I could still smell the leftover traces of Mom's lily-of-the-valley perfume, which had wafted underneath my nose as I ran my hands over the stack of cashmere sweaters on the shelf above my head. Mom loved cashmere so much that she wore it even in the summertime. Dad and I had given it to her as a gift every birthday, Christmas, and Mother's Day for as long as I could remember. By the time of the accident, it seemed like Mom owned a cashmere sweater, scarf, and pair of socks for every colour of the rainbow.

I had taken this sweater down and pulled it over my head, letting the smell and feel of Mom take over. And that was when the tears finally started to flow. Months and months of pent-up sadness spilled out of my eyes and down onto the soft lilac knit of the cashmere. I sunk into a puddle on the floor of that closet and cried for my mother and the memories I worried would soon fade away.

"Mommy mommy mommy," I sobbed. As if saying her name over and over again could somehow bring her back. I needed to know when the sadness would go away ... when I would stop seeing her face in crowds

and hearing her voice in my dreams ... when I would start to feel normal again.

And I was still waiting for those answers. It had been over a year since the accident, and my memories of her were slipping further away with each passing day.

"Mack?"

I opened my eyes and looked up into Marla's face, ready for the inevitable look of pity. But instead, for the first time ever, I saw my own pain staring back at me.

"I know exactly how you feel," she said softly. "My mom's dead, too."

My mouth fell open with shock. "Really? When? How?"

She turned her head and nodded towards my window.

"Believe it or not, it happened right down there."

"What?" I gasped, walking over and peering down at the busy intersection below. I turned and looked back at Marla, my face covered in question marks.

"Was it a car accident?" I asked, remembering the frenzied rush of crazy drivers and blaring horns.

"No — a bus bombing," she explained, her pretty face crumpling with sadness. "It was almost four years ago now. We were going to the market together, only we got into an argument about something stupid on our way to the bus stop. I got mad, turned around, and came home. And she got blown up by a terrorist."

Suddenly, Marla stopped talking and bit her bottom lip. I knew right away that she was leaving out her most horrible parts, too.

"Oh my God, I can't believe it!" I whispered, sitting back down on the bed. "That's just so awful!" An icy chill passed over my body, followed quickly by a layer of goosebumps. I rubbed at my arms, trying to smooth them away. "Aren't you angry, Mar?"

She looked surprised at the question. "Of course I'm angry. My mom was murdered, Mack! You, of all people, can understand how that feels. Aren't you angry, too?"

I nodded.

"At one point, I couldn't even leave my house I was so angry," she continued, wiping away a stray tear from the corner of her eye. I could hear the control she was putting into each word, trying to keep her voice from breaking. "For a long time, I wanted to die, too. I used to wish Mom and I had never argued that day — that I'd been with her on that bus. At least that way I wouldn't have to deal with the pain of living without her. It's been almost four years since the attack, but some days I still feel like that."

I saw a couple of big tears roll down Marla's cheeks before she turned her face towards the window. "You know, my mom was a really good person — a doctor, for God's sake. She didn't deserve to die. I mean, just think of all the lives she could have saved if she was still alive."

When she turned back to me her cheeks were soaking wet. She lifted the hem of her T-shirt and began wiping them.

"Oh Mar ...," I started to say, then stopped. I wanted to say something to make her feel better, but I knew from experience that there were no words for that.

"My dad tries to help," she went on with a small sniffle. "He tells me I can't let the guilt and anger and sadness take over my life. He says being angry all the time doesn't solve anything — it just eats away at your insides. I know he's right, but it's still hard sometimes, you know?"

Her voice finally broke on the last word. I reached out to give her a hug. We sat like that for a few minutes, letting our tears fall and thinking about what each other had lost. Finally, Marla sat back and forced out a shaky smile.

"Hey listen, do you ever go up to the rooftop?"

I shook my head. "No, what are you talking about?"

She stood up and flung off her sadness like a heavy winter coat. "All these buildings have access to the roof. Let's go up and look at the view."

In less than a minute, she located the access door and we were on our way up. When we got to the top of the stairs I gazed around in amazement. It was beautiful. A sunny terrace with plants and deck chairs, solar panels, and, even though it was only four stories high, a great view of the huge, sloping Mount Scopus. I couldn't believe I'd been here for eight weeks and not discovered it myself.

It was already late in the afternoon, the sunlight was dusty and soft, and we had nowhere else to go, so we stretched out on the chairs and watched the sun go down. We talked about our mothers and shared some of our best memories. It was the first time I'd been able to do that without an unbearable ache taking over my body. I even found myself laughing once or twice.

I told Marla about Mom's obsession with cashmere, how she always sang in the car to help cope with her phobia of driving, and how she used to make pancakes on Sunday mornings and pour them into the shapes of all my favourite storybook characters.

"Cinderella, the Big Bad Wolf — she could do them all!" I said proudly.

And Marla told me about when she and her mother used to go to restaurants in Buffalo and pretend not to speak any English to see who could make the waiter laugh first. And how after they moved to Israel, they would sometimes rent a car and take off on "girls-only" weekend drives through the desert.

For the first time in ages, my aching heart came out of hiding. And it felt good. When the sun finally went down, the cool evening breeze made the air feel almost like a summer night in Toronto. And the moon rising over the mountain and the endless ceiling of stars hanging overtop was an incredible sight to see. We stayed up there until we saw Dad's car pull into the parking lot below.

"C'mon," I said, taking Marla's hand and pulling her out of her chair. "I'll introduce you to Einstein himself."

Then I took Marla downstairs to meet him.

Chapter 8

∿∿∿

It was nighttime on the Judean Plain. The lights from the city shone on the horizon, illuminating the site with a soft grey glow. Nasir and Baba were stretched out on the ground, digging in the dry earth. Beside them, a metal detector and a pickaxe lay in the sand and a pair of flashlights pointed towards the hole they were gradually enlarging with their trowels. Keeping their heads down, they dug slowly, taking their time and watching their work with close attention. Nasir tried not to let his feelings of disapproval show on his face. Although his father had explained the "job" to him during the drive out here, he still couldn't believe they were actually going through with it.

No wonder he didn't want Mama to know what he was up to, Nasir thought. He understood that his relatives were struggling, but he knew there had to be a better way to get money than this! Maybe he could ask for more hours at the store ... or look for a second job ... or something.

"Tell me again what we're looking for, Baba," he whispered, trying to keep his words from sounding like a complaint. After almost an hour of digging, his throat was dry and his arms were getting tired.

Baba didn't lift his eyes from his work for a second. "Coins, jewellery, ancient cooking utensils — anything like that," he replied, tossing a clump of dirt to the side.

Nasir swiped a stream of sweat off his forehead with the back of his hand and waited another minute before asking the question that had been on his mind all night.

"But Baba," he asked, choosing his words carefully, "isn't this kind of thing against the law?"

His father stopped digging and looked up. Even in the darkness, Nasir could see the flash of anger in his eyes. He knew he'd said the wrong thing.

"Against the law?" Nasir's father repeated, pointing the tip of his trowel at his son like an accusing finger. "The law says that everything pulled from this earth belongs to the state of Israel. But that's not true, Nasir. You must remember that it belonged to *us* before it belonged to *them*. This is our heritage and we have every right to claim it. Give it to Israel? Who needs it more, your poor grandparents and aunt who are suffering in a refugee camp, or the rich government? Just remember, we wouldn't be here right now if *they* hadn't driven us to this point."

He was practically daring Nasir to disagree with him. But Nasir knew enough not to argue with his father when he got angry. Not when it was about politics or religion. And especially not when it was about the Palestinian cause. Nasir scooped up a handful of dirt and let it fall slowly from his trowel. Sometimes it was hard for him to believe how much violence had been waged over such a dusty, dry stretch of soil. Ever since he could remember, his father had told the story of how the Palestinians had been robbed of this land. Baba had often spoken of *al-Nakba*, the catastrophe that befell their people when Israel became a nation. But Nasir's textbooks at school told a different story. From them, he'd learned that the Arabs and the Jews *both* had roots here. It was a fact he was wise enough not to point out to his father right now.

"But ... but Baba, I still don't understand how we're going to sell it," he said instead. "I mean, who's going to buy an ancient fork ... or frying pan ... or whatever we find out here?"

"Just keep digging," he replied, pointing his trowel back down to the hole. "And let me worry about those details."

After that, neither of them said much. It was really late now — just a few more hours until sunrise, when Nasir knew he'd be pulled from his bed for the morning prayers. He worked diligently, telling himself how every shovelful of dirt was bringing them closer to finding something for Baba and getting him home to his bed. They carried on with their digging for another hour until Nasir's shovel struck something with a loud *clang*. Baba immediately grabbed his flashlight and shone it into the hole.

"You've found something Nasir!" he cried, reaching down the hole to remove the object from the ground. Baba gasped when he saw what it was: a small figurine, no bigger than a child's hand. He gently brushed the dirt away, slowly revealing the bronze image of a woman draped in a long, flowing robe.

Nasir sat back on his heels and sighed with relief. He had no idea how old this thing was and didn't really care, either. They'd found what they'd come for — although neither of them dared utter a peep of celebration out there in the darkened field.

While his father looked over his prize, Nasir gazed up at the full moon floating over Mount Scopus. To him, it looked like a giant eye staring down from above — a colossal-sized witness to their crime.

Chapter 9

∿∿

Have you ever been the new kid in school? Pretty scary, right?

Well, try being the new kid in school in a completely different country with classes in a completely different language. I realized quickly that it was time to sink or swim! The first day was absolutely hellacious — by the end of it I needed a life jacket.

My homeroom was a nightmare — nobody said a word to me except for the teacher, but even that was only during roll call. In between classes, I walked the halls like a geek, staring at my shoes and clutching the straps of my backpack for dear life. Call me paranoid, but I could feel their eyes on me, the freaky new girl with the pasty white skin.

Thank God Marla was there with me. Even though she was one grade ahead, at least we got to meet up at lunchtime. Honestly, if I had to spend lunch sitting by myself I would probably throw up!

The first day she introduced me to some of her friends.

"This is Mackenzie Hill," she said, putting a protective arm around my shoulder as we joined them in the cafeteria. "She just moved here from Canada and she's going to sit with us from now on. Okay?" She spoke in English. I had already figured out that all the kids at my school spoke English outside of class. *Thank God for small favours!*

"Um, hi." I smiled, hoping to look friendly ... but not overly friendly like I was trying too hard. One thing I learned from my old high school is that nobody likes a desperato.

The three girls looked up from their cellphones, waved hello, and made room for us at the table. There was Ronit, a short girl with curly brown hair who seemed kind of shy. I wasn't sure if I liked her or not. Even though she didn't say much, I got a creepy feeling from her, like she was judging me or something.

And there was Yael, who I did like right away. She was bubbly and cute and always seemed to be smiling with her dimples and gap-toothed grin.

And there was Noa with the smoky grey eyes. She was curvaceous, beautiful, and radiated confidence. I could tell right away that she was the kind of girl other girls watched and tried to copy.

For the entire first week, they were the only kids in school who spoke to me. The five of us sat together every day for lunch. On the rare rainy day we stayed in the cafeteria, but most of the time we would take our food outside and sit under the shade of the giant olive tree and talk.

Well actually, *they* would talk and I would listen.

Holy cow! The kids in Israel might look and dress the same as the kids back home, but they sure didn't act the same. Yeah, they were interested in dating and clothes and movies, but the things that really got them excited were politics, social matters, world affairs, and religion. They were so ultra-intense it was almost frightening.

Every day there were heated discussions and some-times even arguments. And it wasn't just Marla and her friends. Walking down the hallway was like elbow-ing your way through a debate club meeting.

Right wing ... left wing ... conservative ... liberal ... moderate ... Orthodox ... reform. Everybody, and I mean *everybody* here had an opinion about something. Everybody, that is, except me.

I watched and listened, but I honestly didn't know what to think. One side would say something and it would make sense, but then the other side always had some good points and, in the end, I was just confused. They all wanted to know where I stood, but I'd never even considered most of this stuff before.

Back in Canada, I used to catch the occasional news story and sometimes even Larry King when I was flipping channels on TV. I had been vaguely aware of what was going on, but to tell you the truth, the troubles of the world had just been like background noise. Sure, it looked bad when I took the time to watch, but it was almost always happening on the other side of the globe. Now it was here in my own backyard ... and I was quickly learning that staying neutral was not an option.

I confided my feelings to Marla on the way home from school one day.

"It's like it's a crime not to have an opinion around here!" I complained.

"Yeah, well, that's the way it is in this country. I was the same as you when I first moved to Israel."

"Really?" That surprised me. She seemed so out-spoken and sure of herself.

"Absolutely. It's like, why concern yourself with

the problems of the world when your life is so far removed from it, right? But here in Israel, you're in the middle of it all. You're involved because of your address, whether you like it or not."

"I don't know," I mumbled. "I guess I'm just not an in-your-face kind of person."

She smiled and patted me on the shoulder. "That won't last long here. It's good to have your own opinions. You can't always let other people tell you what to think."

We walked in silence for a minute.

"Anyway, I wouldn't worry about changing right away," she added, her voice a sing-song of secrets.

"Why not?"

"Well, for now, what you're doing seems to be working for you in the guy department."

"What do you mean?" I stopped walking and grabbed her arm. "What guy department?"

"I mean," she explained, turning to me with a funny little smirk, "that from what I hear, the guys at school are fascinated by you. They all want to know why you don't talk."

I couldn't believe my ears!

"I don't talk because I don't know what to say!" I said defensively.

"Maybe so, but they think you're hiding a deep secret or something. You're getting a reputation around school as, I think the words I heard were, 'some kind of mysterious, exotic beauty.'"

"What? Me? Exotic? A beauty?" I almost choked on the words.

"Yes you!" she laughed. "Is that so hard to believe? Haven't you noticed guys staring at you?"

"Yeah ... but ... but I thought it was because they thought I was a geek."

"Well, Mack, think again! You're a really pretty girl — don't you realize that?"

I didn't. So I have to admit, I was very flattered to be thought of as exotic. Back in Toronto I had always felt like such a plain Jane.

Later that night I stared at myself in the mirror for a long time, examining my features. *Was* I pretty? Had I changed at all since the move? It was hard to tell.

I wondered about the boys at school and which ones had noticed me. The short guy who was always asking to borrow my pencil in math class? The cute one with the baseball cap whose locker was right next to mine? The one with the glasses who'd smiled at me on my way into the cafeteria earlier that day?

After a while I stopped trying to figure it out and went to bed. Because in the end, it didn't really matter. There was only one boy I wanted to impress.

Chapter 10

◠◠◠

Nasir got a letter from his cousin Ziyad today. Mama was eager to tell him about it when he got home from work. Dropping her stirring spoon onto the counter, she practically skipped across the kitchen to give it to him.

"Thanks," he mumbled, taking it from her outstretched hand and tucking it into the back pocket of his jeans.

"Come, why don't you open it now?" she asked, sounding disappointed.

Nasir would rather have read it alone, but he really had no choice. He knew if he refused, his mother would wonder why. Reluctantly, he pulled the letter back out of his pocket and slowly tore open the envelope. She scooped Baby Rana up into her arms and waited patiently to hear what her favourite nephew had to say.

Mama wasn't the only one who adored Ziyad. He was pretty much the star of the whole Hadad family. Not only was he good-looking and full of personality, he was also a certified genius. He had left to go to university in America a couple of years ago with a full scholarship to study engineering at MIT. Growing up together in Jerusalem, the cousins had always been really close. Nasir idolized Ziyad — he considered him to be the older brother he never had. The summer before he left for MIT, they used to go up to the rooftop and talk all night about everything from soccer and girls to religion and their dreams for the future. Ziyad was always bursting with new and interesting ideas. He'd really helped Nasir look at the world in a different, more modern way — a way that neither of their traditional families would ever approve of. And the letters he sent from America were no different. But as much as Nasir looked forward to getting them, he always destroyed them immediately after reading them. He couldn't take a chance that his parents would find them — Mama didn't read English, but Baba did.

He unfolded the single-page letter and read silently.

Nasir,

Have you spoken to your parents yet? Are you coming to visit? I know the ticket is expensive. Soon I'll make enough money to fly you over. Once you come you'll never want to leave. I'll get an apartment with a room just for you. I swear, you'll love it here. You're free to do what you want. Right now I'm saving up to buy myself a car. Everyone here drives a car.

How are my parents? Do you see them often? I can tell from their letters that they're growing nervous. They keep asking me to promise I'll return to the Middle East when my degree is complete. Their last letter was about setting up a marriage to one of their friends' daughters in Beirut. They think that will keep me close. But I won't do it.

I'm in love, Nasir — the real thing this time. The women here are so beautiful. And they're free to speak their minds — and marry whoever they please. Everything is so different here. There are jobs here that pay more money in one year than our fathers ever made in their whole lives. You must come join me.

Write to me soon,
Ziyad

"Well?" urged Mama, shifting Rana from one hip to the other. "What does he say?"

Nasir scrambled to come up with something.

"Um ... he says he's well. School is fine and he's studying very hard and earning top marks. And, uh ... he's lost some weight — Western-style food still doesn't please him."

He studied his mother's face, hoping the mention of food would distract her from asking more questions. It worked.

"Ah! Poor child!" she said, clucking her tongue. "What he needs is a big plate of my musakhan. It was always his favourite." Picking the letter out of her son's hands, she frowned as her eyes scanned the page. Nasir held his breath and waited.

"Such a good boy, Ziyad. You should try to be like him when you grow up," she said, handing him back the letter.

He nodded and stuffed it back into his jeans pocket. His thoughts flashed to the gum girl.

"I'll try, Mama," he replied, heading straight for the bathroom where he could read the letter one more time in private before ripping it up and flushing the pieces down the toilet.

Chapter 11

~~~

We spoke! Oh my God! We spoke!

I stumbled up the street towards my apartment, praying my legs wouldn't give out on me. My head was spinning, my heart was racing, my lip was sweating and there was a hot, prickly feeling making its way up the back of my neck. I felt like I was going to faint. I sat down on the curb outside my building and put my head between my knees, willing myself to calm down as my mind went over the details of what had just happened.

Relax, Mack ... relax! Get a grip on yourself!

But I couldn't relax. I was a mess. A quivering, sweating, hopelessly romantic mess. The Arab boy and I finally spoke. Actually, we did more than speak: we touched. Well, he touched me. Oh my God, just thinking about it was making my stomach do flip-flops!

It all started out so normal. I walked into his store, picked out my usual pack of gum, and took it up to the counter to pay. I could feel those brown eyes of his studying me as I fished around in my purse for some money.

Wouldn't you know it, I couldn't find any! Between my new daily habits of coffee and gum I was practically penniless. *Note to self: ask Dad for raise in allowance.* I stood there like an idiot, burrowing furiously in my pockets for change while my face turned red with mortification.

After a few more seconds, I found some shekels at the bottom of my back pocket and sprinkled them on the counter in front of him. I waited for him to take them and put them in his cash register — but he didn't. I pushed the coins closer towards him and cleared my throat.

We did this routine every day — what was he doing?

I racked my brain to think of something clever to say when suddenly he glanced around to see if anyone was watching, then leaned over the counter towards me.

"I see you in here a lot. You buy a lot of gum."

My heart skipped in my chest. His voice was deep and smooth and, although he spoke with an accent, his English was perfect. Just like I'd imagined it would be.

"Um, well — it's sugar-free, so my dentist doesn't mind," I stammered stupidly.

Great, Mack! Why don't you tell him about your last fluoride treatment while you're at it?

He didn't say anything; he just stared at me. Damn it! He must think I'm an idiot.

"Um, my name's Mackenzie," I said to ease the silence.

"Mack-en-zie," he repeated. The way he said it sounded more like "Muck and Zee," but I didn't dare correct him. It was kind of cute.

"Nice to meet you, Muck-and-zee," he said, flashing a smile of beautiful white teeth. "I'm Nasir. Nasir Hadad."

"Hi," I said shyly, willing my face not to blush a second time.

"Do you live in the neighbourhood?"

"Yeah, in the apartment around the corner. How did you know?"

Now it was his turn to look embarrassed.

"I — I just see you in here so much," he stammered.

"Yeah, well, we just moved here from Canada."

His eyes lit up. "Ah! Canada — I have a cousin going to school near there!"

"Oh really?" I laughed. *Did everyone in this country have a cousin in Canada?*

"He goes to university in a big city where the winters are very cold," Nasir continued. "He's been there two years now."

"Is it York University in Toronto? Because my dad's a professor there. Maybe he knows him."

I was eager to find something in common with him. I'd always heard that couples who were destined to be together could find strings of coincidences linking their lives to each other.

Nasir smiled and shook his head. "No, I don't think that's it."

Damn it! So much for destiny!

"Ziyad's school is in Massa... uh, Massa..."

"Mississauga?"

"No, Massa... Massa-twoshits."

I giggled. "You mean Massa*chusetts*?"

He nodded enthusiastically. "Yes. His school is called MIT — it's a very difficult school. Ziyad is very smart. You said your father's a professor? He must be a very smart man, too."

"Yes, very smart," I agreed, unsure what to say

next. I didn't want to talk about Dad. And I didn't want to embarrass Nasir by telling him that Massachusetts was like, a ten-hour drive from where I lived. I cleared my throat again and hoped I would come up with something funny that would make him laugh and realize how witty and friendly I was. But my mind drew a blank. So instead I flipped my hair off my shoulder and tried to pose prettily like I'd seen Hailey and Steffi do so many times. It felt kind of awkward, but I hoped it looked good. It always seemed to work for other girls.

Nasir leaned forward a little more until we stood so close, I could hear his breathing over the hum of the ceiling fan. He smelled nice — like fresh laundry and toothpaste. For a split second I thought for sure he was going to kiss me. I hesitated while my brain toyed with the possibility.

Is this too early for kissing? Should I let him or should I push him away? What would Hailey Winthrop do in this situation?

I knew the answer even before I finished forming the thought. *She'd kiss him.*

I closed my eyes, opened my lips, and waited. But then he spoke instead.

"Is your skin real?" he whispered. "Can I touch it?

My eyes flew open. Was he joking? I was used to people teasing me about my skin, not asking to touch it. I smiled and waited another second for him to laugh — but he didn't. He *was* serious.

"Um, okay." I nodded slightly and held out my arm. But instead, he reached for my cheek. I gasped softly as his fingertips connected with my skin. I know it sounds totally cheesy, but the best word I can use to describe how it felt is *electric*.

His hand lingered there. I could feel his fingers trembling as they rested on my face. I wanted to tell him that it was all right. That he didn't have to be nervous. That he could keep them there for as long as he wanted. But I'd lost my voice. And I'd lost my senses, too.

Suddenly, the door opened and a customer walked into the store. Nasir tore his hand away, scooped up the shekels on the counter, and practically hurled them into the cash register. He looked so guilty, like a kid caught sneaking cookies before dinner.

"You'd better go!" he whispered, pushing the package of gum towards me.

I felt guilty, too, even though I wasn't exactly sure why. I nodded, turned on my heels, and fled out the door, up the street, and to the steps of my apartment.

My cheek was still tingling on the spot where he'd touched me. I couldn't get his face out of my head.

Ohmygodohmygodohmygod!

Slowly, I lifted my head up from my knees and took a long, deep breath. I thought about the return ticket I still had tucked away in my room upstairs. The three-month mark of our move to Israel was just two days away.

And then I thought about those incredible brown eyes. And the feel of his fingers on my face.

Okay ... so maybe I'll hang around this country a little bit longer.

Chapter 12

∿∿∿

The date came and went without so much as a word. Dad was so focused on his upcoming archaeological dig that I think he forgot about our deal. Lately all he wanted to talk about was bones and dirt and pickaxes. And you thought *your* parents were weird!

The dig was scheduled for the first three weeks of November. I had mixed feelings about leaving for so long, but Dad didn't give me much choice. When I tried to suggest staying here in Jerusalem with Marla and her family, I got the same old "we're going to stick together, damn it" speech that I got in Toronto, so I knew it was hopeless.

And I couldn't even use school as an excuse. Wielding his professor status, Dad pulled some strings and arranged for me to get an academic credit for helping on the excavation.

"You'll see, Mack — you'll love it," he promised. But seriously, I had my doubts.

Early the next Sunday morning, we took a bus north to Tiberias. The first part of the drive was through the Judean desert. The sand was everywhere. And the road was dusty and dry; my throat was parched just looking at it. I kept my eyes glued to the window, watching the sand — the vastness of it was mesmerizing. All I could think about was how easy it would be for a person to just disappear out here in this desert wasteland and be lost forever.

When we arrived, we settled into the hotel and met the rest of the group. I hadn't realized what a big deal this dig was. In addition to the students from the university, volunteers from all around the world had come to help out. There were backpackers from Australia and New Zealand, a middle-aged husband and wife from England, a group of friends from Italy, a father and son from the US, and a tour group of twentysomethings from Montreal.

There was even one grandmotherly woman from Iceland who said it had been her lifelong dream to be here. And a newly married couple from South Africa who had come here for their honeymoon.

A lifelong dream to dig in the dirt? Honeymooning

with a shovel and bucket? Seriously?

Needless to say, they were all gung-ho about getting to work. But I have to admit that it took me a few days to wrap my head around this place ... and even longer to get used to the early hours.

Every day we were woken up at five o'clock in the morning, given a light meal of coffee and cake, and bused to the site. Digging usually ended each day by two in the afternoon.

Now, I'm not normally the kind of girl to pull a princess trip, but I mean, come on — five o'clock in the morning? Can you imagine? I don't care if it *was* the best way to avoid the heat. Plus, the work we had to do was *really* hard! We toiled away in pits of dirt, digging, scooping, sifting, and brushing. Everyone wore hats and sunblock and thick gloves that reminded me of Mom's old gardening gloves. Except unlike Mom's prize-winning roses, the only things growing in this garden were bones and dust.

Man, the air was unbearably dry and dusty. By the end of each day, my muscles were tired and sore and I felt like I'd taken a bath in dirt and sweat.

But the worst thing of all had to be the toilet. Scratch that — it wasn't even a toilet: it was a dingy, smelly porta-potty that was totally gross. The first time

I saw it I wanted to cry. I swear to God, it looked like it hadn't been cleaned since Biblical times. The floor was caked with dirt, the toilet seat crusted with dried urine, and the stench that emanated from that dark, dank hole was practically prehistoric. I swore up and down that I wouldn't use it.

"Ew! I'd rather hold it in all day than sit there!" I complained to Dad, giving him my best "yuck" face.

"Okay, suit yourself," he said with a funny smirk, like he didn't believe me.

But you know the saying — "when you gotta go, you gotta go." Short of relieving myself on Biblical remains, I didn't have any other choice. I quickly learned to hold my breath and pee like lightning.

I could tell Einstein wasn't too thrilled with my attitude. On one of the very first days I unknowingly committed a cardinal sin of archaeology: I picked up a rock. I remember turning it over in my hand, wondering how long it had been lying there. Definitely centuries — maybe even millenniums.

This would be a cool souvenir for Marla, I thought, and I dropped it into my pocket.

A second later, he was at my side.

"Hey Mack, what are you doing? Put that back."

"Why?" I frowned. "It's just a rock."

He sighed and shook his head. "Honey that might look like a regular old rock, but it's not. Everything here is a valuable piece of evidence from the past. That rock might be part of an ancient wall, or it could have writing on it with information and names."

I took it out and looked at it again. It looked just the same as any ordinary stone you'd find in a public park or in someone's backyard.

"Yeah, okay Dad — whatever," I said, letting it fall back down to the ground with a loud *plop*. He sighed and walked away. I knew he was frustrated with me, but I didn't care. After all, it was his big idea to drag me out here in the first place. I'd much rather be back home hanging out with Marla and buying gum from Nasir than digging through piles of old sand.

But everything changed the day I made my first big discovery. It was about a week into the trip and I was sifting through what must have been my hundredth pile of dirt when I felt something hard between my fingers.

"I found something!" I gasped, pulling it from the dirt and dusting it off with my brush.

A surge of excitement shot through me as I realized what it was. A pottery shard. But not just any old regular one: this was a large, fully intact piece. I held it gingerly in my hand like an egg, marvelling at the idea that I was the first person to touch this thing in two thousand years. After we washed it, we found that it had writing on it, too. Apparently, that was a pretty big deal.

"Great job, Mack!" cheered Dad. "Somebody get this girl an ice cream!"

I could see the pride in his eyes. You know, the look parents get like "one day you're going to grow up and be just like me." I have to admit, I was proud of myself, too. I walked around feeling like the Queen of Archaeology for a while. But the very next day, somebody else had an even bigger find and knocked me off the throne. It was a stash of ancient silver coins found wedged under a loose stone in one of the floors. News of the find buzzed through the site as Dad gathered everyone around to have a look.

"A stash of coins hidden under the floor. Can anybody imagine what they were doing there?"

We all took a moment to consider the possibilities, but nobody spoke up.

"Well," he continued, "if it was just one coin, we would conclude that it was dropped accidentally and forgotten. However, an entire hoard of coins suggests that somebody put them there deliberately. The question is, who? Does anybody want to put forth a theory?"

He paused again while we all looked at each other nervously, wondering who was going to speak first.

"Don't worry, there's no wrong answer," he laughed. "Which is exactly what I find so fascinating about archaeology: it's all a big puzzle. Our task here is to rebuild lost civilizations. How do we do that? By using these ancient fragments from the earth, a bit of history, and a dash of imagination."

Dad's eyes sparkled as he spoke. I don't think I'd seen him this alive since before Mom's accident.

"So, how did these coins get here?" he asked again, holding one up for inspection. "Let's take ourselves back to Biblical times when this dirt beneath our feet was a thriving metropolis. Maybe a slave was secretly pilfering them from his master. Or perhaps a desperate merchant hid his savings from the menace of an approaching army. Or maybe a housewife was hoarding money to keep it safe from her gambling husband. Whoever it was, they hid it here not knowing they would never see it again. Not knowing they'd hidden it so well, their stash wouldn't be found until thousands of years later — by us."

It was incredible. For a split second I felt transported

back in time. And I wasn't the only one. I could tell that the others were feeling the magic of Dad's vision, too.

"You see, the people who lived here were just like you and me," he went on. "Mothers, fathers, daughters, sons, students, teachers, and tradesmen. They worked under this same hot sun every day and gazed up into the same starry sky as you do every night. And this site is the time capsule they've left behind. Everything we find is a clue to decoding the details of their lives."

Cool! In that moment, the whole archaeology thing finally started to make sense for me. I began to understand why a couple would honeymoon here instead of Hawaii. And why a sixty-five-year-old woman would spend her life's savings to be here. It was probably the most amazing thing I'd ever seen. There were ancient cities buried under our feet. I remember thinking that a person could get lost forever out here in the desert.

After that day, I knew it was true.

Chapter 13

ᴍᴍ

Lately, Nasir's ears were always on alert.

He heard the traffic noises suddenly grow louder — he knew that meant the door to the store had opened. Pushing the carton of toilet tissue onto the nearest shelf, he ran out of the stockroom to see if it was Mackenzie. It wasn't. Instead, a young mother struggled through the narrow doorway, pushing a stroller with a newborn baby. Usually he would have run to help. Today he just sighed and turned his face away, trying to hide his disappointment.

Where has she gone? he wondered. It had been two weeks and three days now since he last saw her. He wasn't sleeping well. He often woke up in the middle of the night with his body covered in a layer of damp, sweaty worry, his head jumping with questions.

Has she gone back to Canada? Did he say something

to offend her? Maybe she's become sick?

Leaning over the counter, he picked up a package of her favourite gum and held it tenderly in his hands. He thought about the day he'd touched her cheek and how soft her skin had been. And the way she'd smelled. It was so sweet and fresh ... like a ripe peach. He closed his eyes and took a deep breath through his nose, remembering. The baby in the stroller began to cry. His eyes flew back open.

Stop being so stupid, he scolded himself, tossing the gum back down. *Forget about her! There'll be other girls.*

The traffic roared again and his head swung towards the door. His hopeful heart rose in his chest, but fell back down when an old, balding grandfather hobbled into the store.

He sighed again.

The problem was, he didn't want another girl.

Chapter 14

∿∿

Can you guess what the first thing I did when we got back from Tiberias was?

Unpack my suitcase?

Nope.

Take a long shower?

Uh-uh.

Call Marla?

Wrong again.

Run down the street to buy a pack of gum from Nasir?

Exactly!

Okay, I admit I was a little bit obsessed. But it's not like I'm some kind of crazy stalker or anything — I just needed to see him.

So imagine how my teenage heart soared with joy when he looked happy to see me, too. Happy, and quite a bit relieved.

More than anything, I wanted to run over and tell him where I'd been and apologize for leaving without saying goodbye. But I had to stop myself — I knew he wouldn't talk to me while there were other people in the store. I glanced around; there were two other customers cruising up and down the well-packed aisles. Parking myself next to the potato chips, I gave them all the hairy eyeball and silently willed them to get out.

Five minutes later I got my wish. I hurried up to the counter before anybody else walked in.

"Muck-and-zee! Where have you been?" Nasir asked, flashing me that great white smile.

"I went on a trip with my dad to Tiberias — an archaeological dig, actually."

"Oh, really?" he replied, his smile fading a little. "Did you find anything?"

"Yeah, a few pottery shards, a bunch of coins, and some old bones. It was cool."

"Cool," he echoed. Those eyes of his were practically glued to my face. I'd almost forgotten how intense he could be. Suddenly, I felt a little bit warm.

"Well ... uh, anyway ... I'm back now," I managed to squeak.

"I'm glad. This whole time I was worried you were buying your gum somewhere else."

"No way, I wouldn't do that," I mumbled shyly. Beads of sweat were beginning to form on my lip. I prayed he wouldn't notice.

"Listen, I shouldn't be doing this," he whispered, leaning a little closer.

I turned and looked over my shoulder; there was nobody else in the store.

"Doing what?" I whispered back. "And why are you whispering?"

"I want to talk to you. Do you want to meet me after work? I get off early tonight."

I was suddenly so hot, my clothes felt like they were melting.

"Oh, um ... sure!" I said quickly, before he could change his mind.

"Great. But don't come here — meet me at Emek Refaim at eight-thirty. I'll be waiting in front of the Aroma coffee shop."

"Okay."

Behind me, I heard the door open and a new customer walk in. Nasir reacted with a startled jump and then immediately turned away and began fiddling with the cash register. I hurried out of the store, not daring to say goodbye. I spent the entire walk home wondering how on earth I was going to get Dad to agree to this.

It wasn't until I got to the apartment that I noticed I'd completely forgotten to buy any gum.

Chapter 15

~~~~

Nasir pulled his last clean shirt down over his head then ran a hand through his tousled hair. He'd been saving the shirt for work tomorrow, but now tonight's date was way more important.

A date! he thought. *I'm going on my first date!*

His stomach churned with nerves as he thought about the night ahead. He'd never done anything like this before. Would he hold her hand? Would he touch her cheek again? Would they kiss?

Nasir grabbed on to the edge of the sink to steady himself. He'd never kissed a girl before and his stomach felt like it was being turned inside-out just thinking about it. Maybe he and Mackenzie would just talk instead. But what would they talk about? Would they have *enough* to talk about? *She might not know about soccer*, he thought. *What sport do they play in Canada? Isn't it ice hockey?*

With shaking hands, he dabbed on a small splash of cologne from a bottle he'd borrowed from the store. After making sure the lid was screwed back on tight, he glanced around the tiny bathroom for a place to hide it. After a minute, he lifted the top of the toilet tank and carefully deposited the bottle inside. Nasir knew it wasn't the best place for cologne, but with no room of his own, he didn't have much choice. With one last careful look in the mirror, he hurried out of the bathroom. He was worried if he spent too much time getting ready his parents might become suspicious.

Dinner was over. Amar and Sameera were in bed and Rana had just fallen asleep in the rhythmic rocking of Mama's arms. Baba was sitting on the couch, crunching watermelon seeds and watching his favourite Lebanese news program. Nasir knew this was his chance to leave without attracting too many questions.

"I'm going to meet some friends — won't be out too late," he said. Avoiding the usual kiss, Nasir made a hasty exit out the door in the hopes his parents wouldn't detect the scent of his cologne. He felt a pang of guilt as he made his way down the stairs — but it wasn't enough to make him change his mind. There was no way he could tell his parents the truth about what he was doing. Sneaking out to meet a girl was bad enough ... but the fact that she was a *Western* girl made it all that much worse. Mama and Baba would never, ever approve.

This wasn't the first time Nasir had ever lied to them. He loved his parents very much and he wanted them to think that he honoured the Islamic ethical code of being a truthful and honest person, but he didn't want to live the life they were planning for him. He didn't want to carry on praying five times a day, every day, for the rest of his life. And he definitely didn't want to be forced to marry a Muslim girl that he didn't know and didn't love. He didn't even want to stay in the Middle East. His friends at school were full of idealism for the Palestinian future. But Nasir was more of a realist than them. He wanted to live in a place where there was a promise of a better tomorrow. He want *his* son to grow up with a room of his own, not a lumpy couch for a bed. He wanted him to hold a soccer ball in his hand, not a shovel. He wanted to follow Ziyad's example. He wanted to choose his own future. And he wanted it to be with someone like Mackenzie.

Just the thought of her brought a silly grin to his face. He'd been so relieved to see her today. He really hadn't known just how much he'd missed seeing her until she walked back into the store.

He arrived at Aroma a few minutes early. He knew he would probably attract too much attention if he tried to wait right in front. *They'll think I'm a suicide bomber or something*, he thought, shaking his head. Already he could see the security guard posted at the door checking him out as a possible threat. Tonight, of all nights, he wasn't looking for trouble, so he walked a safe distance away, squatted on the curb, and watched the crowds of people pass around him as he searched the faces for Mackenzie.

Chapter 16

∿∿

"You're going where?" Marla practically screamed over the phone. "With who?"

"Shhhh ... keep your voice down," I pleaded. She was so loud I was worried that Dad might hear her through the walls. "I'm meeting Nasir at Emek Refaim," I whispered, hoping she would get the hint and follow suit. "I told Einstein that I was going to your house. I need you to cover for me in case he calls."

"But I thought he didn't let you out at night," she said, sounding suspicious. "Isn't seven o'clock your curfew?"

"Yeah, normally it is, but I whined and complained that I haven't seen you in three weeks. I think he felt badly, because he gave in pretty quickly."

"I don't know — I don't like this at all," she clucked in my ear.

"Thanks for your concern, Marla, but I already have one overprotective parent. I don't need another."

"Fine, but you and Nasir are both going to get hurt," she warned. "You *do* realize that this can only end badly, right?"

I couldn't believe she was giving me such a hard time about one lousy favour.

"Fine, whatever," I snapped. "But will you cover for me?"

There was an unnaturally long sigh on the other end of the phone, followed by a pause, and then finally a small, reluctant "Okay."

"Thanks Mar! I owe you!" I chirped, hanging up the phone and running to get dressed. I had no idea if this qualified as an actual date or not, but I wanted to look amazing anyway, just in case Nasir had any doubts about how much he liked me. Digging through my closet and dresser, I scrambled to find something that he hadn't already seen me wear. But, considering how often I'd been in his store over the past three months, that was next to impossible. So in the end, I finally settled on my favourite blue T-shirt — the one I was wearing that day he touched my face.

I was hoping it would be lucky for me again to-night.

"Bye, Dad!" I called out over my shoulder as I ran out the door.

"Goodbye, Mack," he replied, his voice following me down the hallway. "Be back by ten! No later!"

Nasir was waiting for me on the curb in front of Aroma, just like he said he would be. It was so bizarre to see him out in the real world that it took me a couple of seconds to recognize him. I could tell he had made an extra effort to look nice. He had on a fresh shirt and he smelled faintly of cologne — which made his usual scent of laundry and toothpaste even better.

"Hi," he said.

"Hi," I squeaked, so nervous I sounded just like a munchkin from *The Wizard of Oz*. "What a beautiful night," I added, clearing my throat and hoping he'd never seen that movie before.

If he had, he didn't mention anything. He just smiled awkwardly and started walking. We walked up and down the street for what seemed like miles. It was so nice to be out at night. The air was fresh, the heat of the day was gone, and the neighbourhood seemed to come alive after dark. The shops and patios were open, the sidewalks were crowded, and the cafés were jam-packed with people.

We talked the entire time. Now that we were away from the store, Nasir seemed like a different person — more confident and definitely more relaxed. He told me that he was sixteen, he lived with his parents and three sisters, and he went to a mostly Arab high school in East Jerusalem. He told me how passionate he was about soccer and how he'd once considered playing professionally. And he told me how never in his dreams did he ever imagine meeting a girl from as far away and exotic a place as Canada.

There was that word, *exotic*, again. I lapped it up like soft ice cream on a hot day.

"So, you've lived in Israel all your life?" I asked, eager for more information.

"Yes ... I was born here in Jerusalem."

"And how long have you been working at that little store?"

"Oh ... um, on and off for a while," he replied vaguely. "In between school and soccer — you know, just to make some extra money."

Something in his voice gave me the feeling he didn't want to talk about it, so I didn't ask anymore. Maybe I'd made him uncomfortable by asking about his job. Maybe his family was poor and he was embarrassed at having to work for extra money.

Worried that I'd overstepped my bounds on our very first date, I started talking about myself. I told him all about Canada: how cold the winters are, how you can drive for days without reaching a border, how there's a whole season dedicated to maple syrup, how we have bears and moose and beavers and evergreen forests that go on forever and hundreds upon hundreds of freshwater lakes.

I told him about my high school and my old friends and how they used to call me Snow White. I told him about my old house and the neighbourhood where I grew up. I told him about Dad and how goofy he could be and how he's a visiting professor here at Hebrew U. I basically gave him every detail of my life. I was flattered that he was so interested. Every time I stopped talking he'd ask me something else. I definitely never met any other boy like him before. He seemed so genuinely into me and everything I had to say.

"How does your family like it in Israel? What was your house like in Canada? Did you know Avril Lavigne? Did you have your own car there? Do you want to be a professor, too?"

Eager to please, I didn't hold any detail back. I even told him about Mom, which surprised me, since I normally did anything to avoid mentioning her. But opening up to Marla must have really helped. And Nasir was so easy to talk to, it kind of just came out.

By the time I'd finished telling him everything he wanted to know, it was nine-thirty. Our night was coming to an end and there was still one little thing I was itching to find out.

"So, Nasir, let me ask *you* something now." God, I loved hearing myself say his name!

"Sure — anything."

I twirled a thin strand of hair around my finger and chose my words carefully.

"Um, well, why are you so scared to talk to me when you're at work?"

He shrugged. "You know, the Arab community is pretty close. Somebody might tell my family if they saw us together."

"And would that be really terrible?" I asked, although after Marla's reaction I was almost sure I knew what his answer would be.

He confirmed it with a sombre nod.

"They would *never* approve. I'm expected to marry a Muslim girl."

"Marry?" I giggled, trying to lighten up the conversation. "Who said anything about getting married? I'm only fifteen, you know!"

"Trust me, they wouldn't care how old you are," he replied, tossing his brown hair lightly from side to side. "Dating isn't allowed, either ... until you're engaged, that is."

"Oh ..."

"And neither is kissing," he added.

"It's not?" I whispered, feeling my poor heart sink into my shoes. I wanted to kiss him so badly my lips were burning.

"No, it's not."

I was about to ask him how anybody would ever know when he suddenly stopped walking and reached for my hands. I prayed he wouldn't notice my ugly fingernails. *Note to self: stop biting them!*

"But thankfully, I don't believe in any of that stuff," he said, pulling me gently towards him. Before I knew it, his mouth was touching mine. His lips were so soft — I could taste the faintest bit of toothpaste on them, but it was nice. I think he was nervous, 'cause I could feel his hands trembling in mine. And me? My head was spinning, my knees felt weak, and my heart felt like it was going to pound itself right out of my chest. *Could he feel that, too?* I think if he hadn't been holding my hands I might have fallen over. I knew what we were doing was forbidden and yet that was,

strangely enough, a good thing. Like the most dangerous thing I'd allowed myself to do in a long time.

When we finally came up for air, I looked into his
deep brown eyes and felt myself disappearing inside
them.

Just like the desert.

Chapter 17

∿∿∿

Of course, I called Marla and told her all about it the minute I got home. Unfortunately, it was an awkward conversation. There were a lot of uncomfortable pauses on her end of the line when I described our date. And when she did finally speak, I could hear her voice straining to be nice.

"Okay ... Uh-huh ... That's nice, Mack."

For the first time since our move to Israel, I found myself missing my old Toronto friends. *They* would have been happy for me, I was sure of it!

The next day at school, Marla outed my relationship to her lunchtime buddies.

"Guess what, guys?" she announced in a tone that sounded like a big sister tattling on a younger one. "Mackenzie has a boyfriend!"

My face grew bright red as every eye at the table

turned to look at me in shock.

"Wow! Why didn't you tell us?" asked Ronit accusingly.

"Yeah!" Yael chimed in, swatting me on the arm. "Who is it?"

Before I could answer, Noa jumped in with a guess. "I know! It's Ari from your math class, right?"

"Um … no, it's not Ari," I mumbled.

"Shut up! Then who?" demanded Yael.

"Well, you don't know him," I stalled. "He doesn't go to this school."

"Ooh … Does that mean he's a college guy?" guessed Ronit, bouncing up and down with glee. "Oh my gosh! One of your dad's students?"

I looked over to Marla for help, but she just smiled smugly and shrugged. I was on my own.

"Um, his name is Nasir Hadad," I said. "And no, he's not in college. He goes to high school in East Jerusalem."

The entire table suddenly turned quiet. Within seconds, their looks of excitement began simultaneously melting into frowns of disapproval.

"So, he's *Muslim*?" asked Noa, whispering like it was some kind of curse word.

I couldn't believe these people! How could they

object to someone they didn't even know?

"Yes, he is," I replied, feeling very defensive, "and if any of you have a problem with it, tough!"

And then I did something the old me never would have done: I jumped to my feet and stormed out of the cafeteria. God, was I furious at Marla! I knew she was trying to sabotage my feelings for Nasir. But to tell you the truth, I didn't care if she or her friends approved of him or not. All that mattered was how we felt about each other.

Despite all the negativity surrounding us, Nasir and I continued to meet on the sly. I was pretty daring, meeting him after school or sometimes in the evenings if I knew that Dad was working late. It was tricky, but totally worth it. He was like no other guy I'd ever met before.

I know what you're thinking: he's my first boyfriend, so how would I know, right? But he treated me with such respect and he always listened so attentively to everything I had to say. And he told me how beautiful I was every time we were together — even on the days when I felt plain and pale and awkward. He was almost too wonderful to be true — like my own Prince

Charming out of my very own fairy tale. By the time winter arrived my fingernails had grown so long I had to invest in a nail file.

I was falling in love.

Chapter 18

∿∿

The day was switching to evening. Nasir watched his shadow as he walked towards the park, noticing how its stretched-out form was beginning to fade from sight. Over breakfast that morning Baba had asked to meet him after work. He'd said that he wanted his company while he "exercised," but Nasir knew better. He knew it was because his father wanted to talk in private.

He was waiting when Nasir arrived. There was a big smile on his face and crinkles of pleasure lining the corners of his eyes. Nasir's stomach churned and, for a second, he felt like he was going to throw up. He knew without asking that his father had sold the bronze figurine.

Baba took Nasir's arm and together they walked in silence down a narrow, shaded path until they came to a clearing that offered an excellent view of the surrounding area. Only after making certain no one was within earshot did Baba decide it was safe enough to speak.

"Our dealer has come through for us," he said, his voice bouncing with excitement. "He has sold the figurine to a wealthy American collector and has earned us a substantial profit. This morning I went to the bank and sent the money to your grandparents and aunt."

He paused a moment to wait for his son's reaction, but when it didn't come he continued.

"What I'm trying to say is, thank you, Nasir. You've been a big help. If I can count on you one more time, we might even be able to get the family out of Askar. Maybe even bring them here. Or if the Israeli government won't let them in, perhaps we can get them to America. Your cousin Ziyad could sponsor them."

Yes ... after he's finished sponsoring me, Nasir thought. His stomach churned again as he stared down at the grass and tried to sort through his emotions. He felt sick inside whenever he let himself think about that night on the Judean Plain. Despite Baba's attempts to justify it, going back to dig for more artefacts would transform him, at least in his own mind, from an accidental thief into a criminal repeat offender.

On the other hand, it felt good to be able to help his parents and relatives — especially since Nasir felt like he was betraying them daily by sneaking around with Mackenzie. He lifted his head and met his father's eyes; there was more hope in them then he'd seen in years. Nasir sighed. He knew he was destined to become a huge disappointment to his father one day. How could he refuse him now?

"Okay. You can count on me," he said softly.

Baba smiled again.

"Thank you, my son. The dealer says the antiquities market is very hot right now. He wanted to know how soon we could go back for more. Apparently there are some very lucrative sites up north in the Galilee. He says that many of his diggers have been quite successful in that area. Maybe next time we'll try searching out there."

His diggers? Exactly how many people are involved in this racket? Nasir wondered. He wanted to ask but held back, sensing that perhaps the less he knew the better.

Baba put his arm around Nasir's shoulders and pulled him close. "Just think how much money we could earn next time," he whispered. "One more of those little statues could save your grandparents. If we can bring them out of the camp, they could finally get the kind of medical attention they need. They've lived such a hard life, they deserve to end their days in comfort."

Nasir nodded, suddenly remembering Mackenzie's story of Tiberias, a city located in the region Baba had referred to. She'd talked about finding pottery shards and silver coins. He couldn't even imagine how much money Baba's dealer could get for those kinds of things.

He wasn't proud of what happened next. In his eagerness to please his father and help his family, he did something terrible — so terrible that he would look back on that moment with regret for the rest of his life. He felt the words of betrayal form in his mouth and tried to swallow them down before they could do any damage. But despite his best efforts, they flew from his lips like guided missiles.

"I have a friend," Nasir heard himself saying. "Her father is an archaeology professor from The Hebrew University. He recently led a dig in Tiberias, where they found pottery shards and a whole stash of silver coins. My friend says it's known as the 'city of treasures.' Maybe we should try digging there."

Baba's eyes widened at the mention of the silver coins. He was clearly so hungry for another find that he didn't even seem to care that Nasir's "friend" was a girl — something that would ordinarily have prompted a frown of disapproval.

"Thank you, Nasir. Maybe you can speak to this girl again and try to find out some exact locations. If you can learn more, we might get compensated for the information. But be careful: nobody must suspect what we're doing."

Nasir nodded silently as the impact of what he'd just done began to sink in.

The sound of laughter interrupted his thoughts, providing a welcome distraction from his guilt. He turned his head and saw two boys entering the clearing, kicking a soccer ball. He and Baba stopped talking and watched as the boys approached, running after their ball in the purple light of dusk. They looked joyful and innocent; Nasir guessed that they were only a few years younger than him.

A sudden longing grew in his chest: a longing to leave Baba and go join them in their game. But he knew he couldn't. His head was burdened with secrets and his feet were firmly planted in the adult world of deception and lies.

He wondered how he got to the point where his entire life had become about sneaking around.

After that day, he never played soccer again.

Chapter 19

ᴡᴡᴡ

December in Israel was bizarre. I mean, totally and utterly warped. At least it seemed that way to me.

To start with, it snowed. That's right, snowed! Dad and I must have brought some cold Canadian karma with us across the Atlantic, because one morning early in the month I looked out my window and saw the ground covered with white. I swear, you could have knocked me over with a feather right then and there. If I had known snow in the Middle East was even a remote possibility, I would have brought my ski jacket with me.

The intersection below my window was exploding with honking horns that morning. Man, if you thought the Israeli drivers were crazy in normal weather, you should have seen them skidding around on the wet snow. It wasn't pretty.

Marla showed up on my doorstep an hour later wearing mittens and brimming with excitement.

"Isn't it great?" she gushed. "Doesn't it remind you of home?"

"Um, I guess."

But it didn't really. Back home, the first snowfall had meant the beginning of the Christmas season. Here, it meant nothing.

Forget the bomb shelters and double-flush toilets; my single biggest culture shock from this move had to be the absence of Christmas. It had been Mom's favourite time of year. In the years before the accident, she would spend the entire month of December getting ready for the holidays. Our home would always be decorated with greenery and tinsel and a huge tree and the outside of our house would be covered with strings of tiny, multicoloured lights. Sure, it was hokey, but I liked it. And of course, we weren't the only ones. Malls across the city were adorned with ribbons and garland, carols were blasted 24/7 on the radio, and most of the streets were lit up with Christmas lights.

But there was none of that here in Israel. Heck, we didn't even get a school break.

At least Dad managed to track down a place that sold Christmas trees. But it wasn't the same. One warm

Sunday, we dragged home a straggly looking spruce, propped it up in the living room, and decorated it as best as we could. Not exactly easy considering we'd left all our ornaments back in Toronto with Aunt Louise and Uncle Matt.

"We'll make our own this year. C'mon ... it'll be fun!" Dad urged, showing me how to string popcorn and make garland out of coloured construction paper. "This is how they did it in the 'olden days.'"

I seriously doubted that the pioneers used tinfoil to make their Christmas stars, but I rolled my eyes and went along with it. Really, what choice did I have? We were almost halfway through the year and things were still tense between me and Dad. His pathetic tree just made me miss home. And Mom, too. I knew if she'd been here, she would have found a way to make Christmas special somehow. Dad was trying his best, but his best just wasn't good enough for me. Let's face it: without Mom, we were lost.

And the thirty-first wasn't much different. There was no Dick Clark, no corny singing, and no confetti at midnight. You see, New Year's didn't exist here — at least, not the New Year's I'd always known. The Jewish New Year was celebrated back in September with apples and honey and ram's horns. Called Rosh

Hashanah, it's so different from the New Year's I was used to that I didn't even realize what it was until it was over.

Of course there *was* Hanukkah, which I guess was nice in its own way. I mean, what's not to like about chocolate coins and candles and spinning tops? Marla invited me to her family's Hanukkah party. It was fun, but the smell of frying oil from the pancakes and donuts made me nauseous.

And the snow? It melted after only a couple of hours — just enough time to remind me, yet again, of everything I had lost.

Chapter 20

~~~

Nasir was shocked when Mackenzie brought a camera to the store. She walked through the door, pulled it out of her jacket pocket, and pointed it at him.

"Say cheese!"

Snap.

"What are you doing?" he asked, holding his hands out to stop her. "Please put that away." His eyes flicked nervously up and down the aisles, checking for customers.

"Uh-uh," she replied, skipping towards him and pulling his hands away playfully.

"Smile!" *Snap ... snap ...*

But Nasir was too worried to smile.

"Mackenzie, please!" he repeated.

She sighed softly and lowered the camera down to the countertop.

"Relax. I won't put these pictures up in my room or my locker or anything. I just want one of you for my wallet. Something for me to look at in private ... Okay?"

He hesitated and glanced towards the door. "But what if someone sees us?"

She looked around the store and shrugged. "What are you talking about? There's no one here. And if anyone *does* come in, I'll pretend I don't know you — as usual."

"I don't know, I don't think it's a good idea ..."

But she wouldn't listen.

"Come on ... Don't be so paranoid!" she said, plucking a small bag of potato chips off a nearby shelf and tossing it at his head. "Lighten up!"

"Hey!" he said, ducking away from the flying bag.

"Just trying to get you to smile," she replied, lobbing a package of mints at him.

Her plan worked. When he started laughing, she picked the camera back up, aimed it at him, and shot.

Snap ... snap ...

After that, he began to loosen up. Within a few minutes, he began to like it. He even posed a few times, jumping up on the counter and making funny faces behind the cash register. Nasir couldn't remember ever acting so crazy before. It felt good. Then he had an idea.

"Okay, give me the camera, please," he said, holding out his hand.

Mackenzie raised her eyebrows suspiciously. "Why?"

"I want to take one of you. If you can hide one in your wallet, so can I."

She grinned wide and her face turned red like a tomato. Nasir loved to see her blush. Without hesitation, she handed him the camera and began to get herself ready. He aimed the lens in her direction and watched her in the small viewscreen. She was combing her silky yellow hair with her fingers and licking her lips to make them shine. He watched her longer than necessary, pretending to frame the shot. But really it was a good excuse to stare. He couldn't help himself — she was so beautiful.

When she was ready, she placed one hand on her hip, flipped her hair off her shoulder, and smiled. She held that pose perfectly still. Nasir zoomed in, then zoomed back out. He was stalling, holding her image in his hands, forcing her to wait. As his finger hovered over the shutter button, he realized something about the girl on the other end of the lens. Even though he was holding the camera, Nasir suddenly felt exposed — but in the best way possible. Mackenzie saw him — really saw him, understood him, and believed in him in a way that nobody else ever had before. With all the lies circling around his life, she was the truest thing he had going. He would never let her go — no matter what his parents said.

His eyes rose from the viewscreen and met hers. He wanted to tell her what he was feeling, but didn't know where to start. His mouth dropped open, the words formed on his tongue, but in the end, nothing came out. Mackenzie shifted her weight from one foot to the other and cleared her throat impatiently.

"Okay ... I'm ready, Nasir," she mumbled, lips still frozen in their smile.

His eyes shifted back to the screen. He pushed the shutter button.

Snap.

And greedily took another and another.

Snap ... snap ...

When they had filled the memory card, they chose their favourite shots and Mackenzie left to print them at a nearby camera shop. Nasir waited impatiently for her to return. The idea of hiding her picture in his wallet and looking at her face whenever he wanted was thrilling.

It didn't stay in his wallet for long, however. That night after his parents and little sisters had gone to bed, he brought it out. The room was dark, but as his eyes adjusted to the light he could make out her face and her glowing white skin. When he finally felt himself drifting off, he slipped it carefully under his pillow to keep it safe.

He dreamed great dreams of their future together.

Chapter 21

ᴧᴧᴧᴧ

It happened on the sixteenth of January — the day we skipped school and Marla thought it would be a kick to go shopping in the Arab souk.

That was the day that changed everything.

"So, are you sure it's safe to be there on our own?" I asked as we bounced up and down in our seats on the bus to the Old City. Over the past few months the two of us had been all over Jerusalem and I'd long ago given up any qualms about dying a violent death at the hands of a terrorist. But today I just couldn't get those early words of warning from Dad's professor friend out of my head.

You're in the Middle East, now — a long way from North America. There are people and places in this city that can be dangerous for young girls on their own.

But Marla didn't seem worried at all. "Of course

it's safe," she assured me. "You've been there before, haven't you?"

"Yeah, but Dad was with me."

"Don't worry, it's no big deal as long as we stick together. Trust me, it'll be fun. We'll get some good bargains."

Still, I was nervous. I couldn't shake a nagging feeling that this was a mistake.

We arrived and began making our way through the winding streets of the market. Marla knew exactly what she was looking for.

"Today I want to get a purse, a pair of sandals, and some new earrings," she declared as we poked around in the stores. "What about you?"

I shrugged.

"I don't know. Maybe I'll just look around."

As we walked, Marla gave me some tips on how to haggle for the best prices.

"It's like an art form here, so pay attention. Never look too interested in anything. And never ever *ever* accept the asking price," she warned. "The asking price is only for fools and suckers. Counter with half and always be prepared to walk away."

Wow, she was fierce!

We stopped at several shops while she bargained

with the sellers for the best price. I watched over and over again as both sides passed their offers back and forth — like tennis players in a professional match. Each transaction seemed to follow a similar formula — a cycle of haggling (where friendly banter was followed by discussion of price, which was quickly followed by hurt looks and gasps of indignation) repeated several times until a deal was finally reached.

By the time we were preparing to leave the souk an hour later, Marla got everything she wanted. But I still hadn't found anything to buy.

"So, aren't you going to get *anything*?" she asked, looking a little disappointed that I wasn't keeping up.

I picked up a beaded necklace from a nearby stall, held it up to my neck for a second, then put it back down. It's not like I didn't have any money. Actually, since I stopped buying gum every day I'd been able to save a little. I just didn't know if I was ready to be broke again so soon.

"I don't know." I frowned. "Dad's fiftieth birthday is coming up next week, so maybe something for him. Or maybe a little present for Nasir."

She smirked at the mention of his name. "What about buying yourself a veil?" she asked. "He'd love it, I'm sure."

I walked past her, pretending not to hear. As much as I loved Marla, it seemed like the more time I spent with Nasir, the nastier she got. It was so ironic! After all this time I finally had a boyfriend of my own and I had nobody to talk about it with.

Then it dawned on me: an idea so far out, so ridiculously absurd, I knew deep down it had to be true.

Oh my God — she's jealous!

That had to be it. Just as I was about to call her on it, a man stepped out of a doorway and cleared his throat. He had close-set eyes and a high forehead that made his face appear unusually long. His nose was slightly bulbous and underneath it sat a bushy moustache that was in desperate need of a trim. Although he was smiling, he had a look of emptiness in his eyes that immediately put me on my guard.

"Ahem. Good afternoon, ladies. Are you doing some sightseeing?" he asked in a raspy voice that was thick with accent. "Maybe I can offer you some directions."

I could tell right away the man's accent wasn't the usual Middle Eastern variety — it definitely sounded different. European, maybe?

"No thanks," Marla replied politely, grabbing my hand. "We're not sightseeing, we're here to shop."

The man stepped forward and spoke again, his smile widening.

"Shopping? For that junk?" he asked, gesturing towards the neighbouring stores. "Perhaps you'd be interested in a *real* souvenir." He turned slightly and cocked his thumb towards the small, brightly lit shop behind him. "Why don't you come take a look? I've got all kinds of treasures for sale."

I didn't know what to do. This guy looked creepy to me. But obviously Marla didn't share my concerns. The word "treasure" must have caught her attention.

"Um, okay," she replied, dropping my hand and walking past me into the shop. After a moment's hesitation, I followed suit. I could feel the man's eyes following us as we poked around his store, watching us in silence as we browsed the packed shelves. But despite his promise, he appeared to be selling the exact same kind of stuff as every other shop in the souk: prayer beads, rugs, sequined scarves, silver chalices, candles, ceramic mugs, chess sets, leather sandals, cheap watches, and an assortment of batteries — definitely no treasures.

Just as I was about to grab Marla and leave, the man started talking again.

"Are you girls from America?" he asked, leaning against the wall and stroking his moustache.

Marla picked up a small stuffed camel and nodded. "I am ... but she's from Canada."

His smile widened further. "Look, I don't normally do this," he said, walking towards the cash register, "but perhaps you might be interested in something like this."

We watched as he reached behind the counter and pulled out a small white box. He opened it up to reveal a little ceramic bowl sitting on a nest of straw. I leaned closer to get a better look. It was small and chipped and fragile-looking. I could tell instantly that it was old — really old.

"A genuine Israeli artefact. It's authentic, from before the time of Jesus Christ," he said, holding the box as gingerly as one might hold a freshly laid egg.

My heart jumped with excitement. We'd found so many broken shards on our dig in Tiberias, but never an entire piece like this. It was perfect.

"Oh gosh, Dad would love something like that," I whispered to Marla.

Then, without thinking twice, I reached for my wallet.

"How much?"

He kept smiling. "A special price for you: eight hundred shekels."

I gasped. That was more than my allowance for like, two whole months. I was about to say thank you and walk away when I remembered the first part of Marla's advice.

Never accept the asking price. The asking price is only for fools and suckers.

I screwed up my courage, took a deep breath, and shook my head, "no."

"That's too much. I'll give you four hundred," I heard myself say.

His smile widened even more. Boy, he had big teeth!

All the better to eat you with, called out a little voice in the back of my head.

"I'm sorry, young lady, but this bowl is a piece of history," he said. "It's worth much more than that."

"And how do we know that?" Marla piped up beside me. "Do you have some kind of proof?"

"Proof?" he repeated, raising his eyebrows. "For proof you must go to a museum. But their bowls are not for sale. This one is."

He turned his attention back to me.

"Look, I think you're a nice girl. For this genuine Israeli artefact I can give you a special price of seven hundred shekels."

I wavered, unsure what to do next. Should I offer him six hundred? Or should I follow my instincts and walk away? That's when Marla nudged me hard with her elbow. "Stand your ground," she hissed in my ear.

"Sorry, four hundred shekels. Take it or leave it," I repeated, trying to sound like I didn't care. But I did. I really wanted to get this bowl for Dad. "Is it a deal?"

I bit my lip and waited for his answer. For a split second the man's smile disintegrated and his empty eyes narrowed into slits. In that instant, I swear he looked like a snake ready to strike. A small spasm of fear pinched my chest and the little voice in my head called out, *run*! But a moment later the look was gone and his smile was back again. This time, however, I could tell he was forcing it. With a quick snap of his wrist, he closed the lid of the box and handed it to me.

"You drive a hard bargain. The bowl is yours."

My mouth dropped open from shock. That wasn't nearly as hard as I'd thought it would be!

There was only one problem: I definitely didn't have four hundred shekels on me. I did a quick mental calculation of how much I needed.

"Marla, I'm a little short," I whispered. "Can I borrow some sheks? I'll pay you back."

"Sure," she said, passing me her wallet. "Take what you need."

I was grateful for the loan, and yet I couldn't help wondering if she would have been so generous if the present had been for Nasir.

I walked out of that shop with my head held high. I was proud of myself for haggling so successfully my very first time.

Dad's going to love this! I thought as I tucked the box carefully into my backpack.

Little did I know what a huge mess of trouble I'd just bargained for myself!

Chapter 22

Have you ever planned a surprise for somebody? A surprise so big and exciting that you could barely hold it in? Well, I was so excited to give Dad his present that I walked around for the next few days thinking I was going to burst with anticipation. It took all my willpower to hold it in and wait til the morning of his birthday.

"Happy fiftieth, Dad," I said, taking the box out from behind my back and sliding it across the breakfast table towards him. He looked up from his newspaper in surprise.

"What's this, Mack?"

"A present, silly. Did you think I'd forget?"

"No, honey," he said, putting down the paper. "I just ... well, honestly, I just know that I haven't exactly been your favourite person lately."

I didn't know what to say — we both knew it was true. Instead of trying to deny it, I reached over and pushed the present a little bit closer. "Just open it," I said, squirming in my seat. I couldn't wait another minute to see his reaction.

"Okay, okay," he conceded, smiling as he began tearing away at the wrapping paper.

That was another thing Dad and I had in common: we were both present-rippers. Mom, on the other hand, had been a present-peeler. You know, the careful type who took an insane amount of time unfastening the tape and trying to save the paper. For what, I'll never know. It always ended up in the recycling bin, anyway.

Much to my satisfaction, it only took Dad a matter of seconds to unwrap the gift. But when he pulled back the lid of the box and looked inside, it was *me* who got the surprise.

"Wow! This is great, Mack!" he chuckled, lifting the bowl out and putting it down next to his coffee cup. "What a nice reproduction. Where'd you get it?"

It took me a couple of seconds to understand exactly what he meant.

"No, it's *not* a reproduction, Dad. I got it in the souk. The man who sold it to me said it was authentic, from the Bronze Age or something."

Much to my horror he laughed again, this time even harder. "Oh no, Mack! And you believed him?"

You know that feeling you get on an elevator when you start to rise and your stomach drops down to your feet? Well, that's how I felt: like my guts had just fallen into my shoes. That was the moment I realized something had gone horribly wrong.

Sensing my distress, Dad stopped laughing and reached over to pat my hand.

"Oh gosh, I should have warned you about the rip-off artists in the souk, honey," he said, his voice suddenly sympathetic. "I've heard they'll say anything to make a buck! And a young, naive girl must have seemed like the perfect target. How much did you pay for this?"

I didn't want to tell him. All I could think about was the month of allowance that was gone forever. Little by little, an icky, tingly heat was beginning to make its way across my chest and up my neck.

"Ugh! I'm such a loser!" I moaned, burrowing my face in my hands.

"Don't be so hard on yourself, Mack. It's a very convincing copy — only a professional like me would have been able to tell that it wasn't real."

He plucked the bowl off the table and turned it over in his hands.

"Look here, the people who made this knew what they were doing. See ... It's been fragmented in just the right places to look authentic, and over here the paint has been faded and chipped to make it appear as though it was buried in the ground, and the surface of the pottery appears pebbled and worn as if ... as if ..."

Dad's voice trailed off into a whisper and his eyes narrowed. Reaching across the table for his glasses, he popped them on and brought the bowl closer for a better look. A moment later, his smile melted away and a look of anger seized his features.

"Dear God!" I heard him gasp under his breath. "It's real!"

I couldn't help grinning. For the tiniest of seconds I felt happy — even a little bit triumphant. *I wasn't tricked after all!*

But the next instant my joy gave way to shock as I watched Dad place the bowl carefully back into its nest of straw, jump up from the table, and start yelling.

"It's real, Mack! God damn it! *It's real!*"

He started pacing around the room, shaking his head in fury. I sat there, dumbfounded. If the bowl was real, why was he so mad? A moment later he gave me the answer.

"I can't believe my own daughter would buy a black-market artefact!" he bellowed. "Didn't you learn anything during our excavation of Tiberias? These things are national *treasures!* Nobody, *nobody* is allowed to own them! And certainly nobody is allowed to *sell* them!"

My mouth fell open with shock as I tried to think of something to say. I couldn't remember a time that I'd ever seen Dad so angry at me.

"Who sold this to you?" he demanded, slamming his hand down on the table.

"I ... I ... I don't know!" I stammered, cowering down in my chair. "It was a man in the souk."

"A man in the souk!" he repeated. "What man? Did you get his name? Did he have a store?"

I shut my eyes and tried to think back to the incident. "Yes, there was a store, but I'm sorry, Dad, I don't remember where it was."

He sighed heavily and raked his fingers through his bushy mop of hair. I could tell he was trying hard to regain his self-control. He took another deep breath and sat back down. When he spoke again, his voice was calmer, but I could still hear the tremble of rage behind his words.

"Listen, Mack, do you realize that this country has a huge black-market trade in antiquities?"

"I ... I don't know what that means," I said, feeling kind of stupid.

"It means that people are digging illegal holes into ancient sites just like the one you and I worked at. But instead of studying the artefacts, they're selling them to dealers who turn around and sell them to collectors and tourists and naive shoppers like you and Marla. These people are stealing pieces of history — it's one of the worst problems plaguing the Middle East right now."

"But ... who are these people?" I asked, trying to remember something about the man who sold me the bowl. "Israelis? Palestinians?"

He shook his head. "This is a huge international operation, Mack. Yes, the diggers are usually local and desperately poor. But the dealers come from all over the world. It's an underground industry worth several billion dollars a year. They're criminals, all of them — plundering this region's cultural treasures like modern-day pirates."

He picked up the bowl and traced his fingers carefully over its clay surface. "This piece should be in a museum, not a private collection. And the man who sold it to you should be in jail."

That icky, tingly heat had now made its way up to

my face and was creeping towards my ears. I reached up to scratch them, but that only made it worse.

"I didn't know that when I bought it, Dad," I whispered, feeling my throat tighten up with emotion. I felt like crying.

Now, normally I would try to pull myself together and stay strong, but a little part of me was wondering if maybe a few tears wouldn't make Dad extend me just a little bit of sympathy. After all, I was an innocent victim here, wasn't I?

I decided to test out my theory and let a couple of tears escape and roll down my cheeks. Unfortunately, Dad seemed unmoved.

"Listen, I'm sure you didn't know it was illegal, Mack," he said, "but that doesn't make it all right. Now, I want you to take me back to the place where you bought this bowl and show me the criminal who sold it to you. I'll handle it from there."

"Take you back?" I gulped, reaching for a napkin to wipe my eyes. "When?"

"Today," he said. "Right after breakfast. There's no time to waste if we want to catch this guy."

"But ... but what about school?"

"You can miss a day of school. This is far more important."

"But don't you have a class to teach?"

"Not today — just paperwork and grading."

"But ... but ..."

"No buts! Go get dressed!"

Wow! He was really mad!

Twenty minutes later we boarded a bus to the Old City. When we arrived, we started searching up and down the winding streets of the souk. Together, we examined every shop in the entire place. But it was like a maze in there. For the life of me, I couldn't find where I'd bought the bowl.

"What did the shop look like?" Dad asked over and over. "And the man who sold you the bowl, did he have any distinguishing features? Any scars? Any funny moles? Was he tall or short? Was he fat or thin? Was he alone, or did he have friends?"

I answered as best as I could, but I swear, all the shops looked the same to me. And all I could remember about the seller were his perma-smile, his creepy, empty eyes, and his raspy voice. I scanned every face in the market that day, hoping to spot this guy and erase that look of disappointment on Dad's face. But after five hours of searching my legs were tired, my feet were aching, and we were no closer to finding him.

Exhausted and discouraged, I begged Dad to give up and let us go home.

"Come on, he's obviously not here," I pleaded. "We can try again another day."

He agreed reluctantly, but didn't say anything to me the entire way back. He didn't have to — I knew exactly what he was thinking, 'cause I was thinking the same thing myself. I'd allowed myself to be duped by a common criminal, I'd personally embarrassed him, and, maybe worst of all, I'd ruined his fiftieth birthday.

Way to go Mack!

Chapter 23

~~~

The very next day Dad turned the bowl over to the Israeli Antiquity Authorities and together we filed a report on the incident. I could only imagine what they were thinking when one of the world's leading experts on archaeology showed up on their doorstep with a stolen artefact purchased by his very own daughter. Needless to say, it was a huge blow to Dad's professional pride. I knew he would have felt much better if he could have handed over the thief as well. But to his credit, he didn't try to make me feel any worse. I got the feeling he wanted to put the whole thing behind us as fast as possible. And that was fine with me! Given the choice, I'd happily never talk about it again — to him, or anybody else, for that matter. I wasn't even going to tell Nasir. I just didn't want him to know I'd been so stupid.

It felt funny keeping a secret from him. I guess that sounds weird, huh? Considering our whole relationship was based on sneaking around. But maybe that's the very reason why we'd been so honest with each other about everything else. Because I'd opened up to him about Mom and the horrible way she'd died, I think it made it easier for him to confide stuff in me, too. He told me about a time two summers ago when he and his cousin Ziyad had snuck off to the beach with a bottle of wine and what a risk that was, considering Muslims were forbidden to drink alcohol. And he told me how he had doubts about living out his life in the Middle East and how every now and then he dreamed of leaving everything behind and running off to Hollywood to be an actor.

As cheesy as that sounds, I have to admit that it made me like him even more than ever. He was *totally* cute enough to be a movie star! And his accent probably wouldn't be a problem — after all, look at what happened to Antonio Banderas!

I told him if he ever ran away he'd have to take me with him. I think he liked that idea. We were definitely getting closer with each passing day. After being together for three months now, Nasir didn't seem nearly as nervous when we were out in public together.

And when he was working at the hole in the wall, he even spoke to me when other people were around — even though it was in a whisper.

But he was still reluctant to introduce me to his family. I wanted that to change. If we were going to have a shot at a future together, I was going to have to meet them.

So, okay, I have to admit that I fantasized about our wedding all the time. There were several different versions that I liked to play out in my head, but the basic theme went something like this:

It was a clear summer day — not too humid or hot. I was dressed in a one-of-a-kind antique, ivory-lace dress with a ten-foot train behind me and a diamond-studded tiara poised gracefully on top of my head. Nasir looked great, too; he was so handsome in his dashing tuxedo and white bow tie.

"I love you Muck-and-zee," he said over and over all day, staring at me with adoring eyes that told me without a doubt that I was the most beautiful girl he'd ever seen. All our friends and family were there, of course. Hailey, Steffi, and Christina had all flown over to be my bridesmaids. And Marla was my maid of honour who'd overcome her intense jealousy with many long hours of hypnotherapy.

In the front row were our families. My dad, wearing a formal, black-satin version of his billowing cape, was seated with Aunt Louise, Uncle Matt, and Nana Pearl — who, as my wedding gift, had promised never to make me eat her disgusting English trifle again.

Across the aisle from them was Nasir's family. His sisters were all dressed in matching pink dresses and his mother and father (who now lovingly referred to me as their "fourth daughter") were clasping each other's hands and crying tears of joy at the sight of their only son getting married to such a wonderful young woman.

It was a great daydream. There was only one fuzzy detail: I could never tell exactly where the wedding was taking place. A church? A mosque? That part was always too blurry to make out. But I did know for sure that we looked like one of the happiest couples I'd ever seen. And I just knew if his parents could meet me they'd be able to recognize that.

One evening when Nasir and I were out for a walk I decided to press him on it. It was the middle of February, but the air was warm enough to stroll without a jacket. That *never* happened in Toronto.

"Come on!" I urged in my sweetest, most beguiling voice. "Your parents will love me. I make a great first impression."

I smiled shyly, fluttered my eyelashes, and waited for his reply. It was amazing how good I'd become at flirting over the past few months. It's like I was somehow channelling the spirit of Hailey Winthrop from all the way across the Atlantic Ocean. Surely Nasir couldn't possibly resist me.

Apparently, he could.

"No, I'm sorry — they're very traditional," he said, shaking his head vigorously. "They would absolutely never approve."

I pouted for a while but he wouldn't change his mind.

"And what about you?" he asked, turning the tables back on me. "I'd love to meet your dad one of these days."

But now it was my turn to shake my head.

"No way! You know that Dad doesn't let me date yet. I swear, if he knew about you we'd both be toast!"

"Toast?" he asked with a small frown of confusion. Actually, the way he said it sounded more like "tossed," which was quite adorable. I couldn't help smiling.

"Yes, toast. You know, as in, 'burned to a crisp'? As in, 'raked over the coals'?"

He stopped walking and spun me around to face him.

"Come on! When are you going to tell him you're old enough to do what you want?" he teased.

I was shocked that he, of all people, could ask that question.

"The same day you stand up to your parents and tell them about li'l ole me and my Christmas stocking," I shot back.

I was trying to be funny, but it didn't work — he didn't even smile.

That was a whole month ago. Since then I'd dropped the topic of meeting his family and had pretty much given up the hopes that my daydream would ever come true.

So you can imagine my shock when I finally got an invitation to go to his house. It happened after school one day in March when I was hanging out at his store, hoping to catch him on a break.

"Good news!" he hissed over the cash register. "My family is out of town for a few days. I've got the apartment to myself!"

My heart gave a little leap of joy.

"Where'd they go?"

"To visit my uncle and his family in Nazareth — they

left this morning. I told them I couldn't go with them because I had too much school work."

He gave me a shy look and added, "I, um, thought it would be a good chance for us to be ... you know ... alone."

My heart leaped again at the thought of getting a glimpse of his home life — even if his family wasn't going to be there. We arranged to meet the following afternoon after school just outside the gates of the Arab souk. I raced back home, certain that the next day would be the most important one in our relationship so far. I'd never been alone in a boy's apartment before and I really didn't know what to expect. Would we talk, or would we just kiss the whole time? Or would we do more than kiss? Up until now, that's all we'd done. Was I ready for more? *Oh God!* Just the thought of it unleashed a swarm of butterflies in my stomach. *I love Nasir ... don't I?* I was pretty sure I did. But did he love me? I didn't know if I wanted to take such a huge step yet. What exactly was *he* hoping would happen tomorrow? What would Hailey Winthrop do? I thought back to the advice she'd given us that day last spring after her date with Harrison Finch. Advice that her big sister had offered to her: *Always leave a guy wanting more.* Oh God! *More what?* I wanted — no, scratch that — I *needed* to talk to somebody about it. Against my better judgement, I called Marla.

"He's invited me over to his house! Isn't that great? Don't you think that's a big step for us?"

I felt kind of like a lawyer trying to sway the opinion of a cranky jury. But it didn't work. Her disapproval came through loud and clear over the phone line.

"I really wouldn't go if I were you, Mack. It's not exactly the safest of neighbourhoods for a girl on her own."

"I won't be on my own — Nasir will be with me."

"I don't know if that's any better," she snorted.

"Ugh! Here we go again! You're my best friend. Why can't you be happy for me?"

"Because I don't agree with what you're doing!" she replied. "I've told you before: the only way for this to end is badly!"

Ooh! I could feel the beginnings of a hot, prickly anger starting to creep across my body!

"You know Marla, not *all* interfaith relationships are doomed," I lectured in my best know-it-all-professor's-daughter voice.

She just sighed wearily, like a parent exasperated with a rebellious child.

"Listen, Mack: all I'm saying is that it's a dangerous idea. I'm *trying* to look out for you, you know."

And that was the proverbial straw that broke the camel's back. I couldn't control my anger anymore. All these months of negativity had brought me to my boiling point.

"God! Why are you such a bigot?" I yelled into the phone.

That did it. Now she was angry, too.

"I'm not a bigot!" she yelled back. "Go ahead and do what you want when you get back to Canada, Mack. It's just *not* the same here. We are at *war* with them! Don't you get it?"

"No, I don't get it! *I'm* not at war with anyone!" I screamed, and I slammed the phone down.

I sat there shaking with anger, wishing I hadn't called at all. How dare she talk to me like that? How dare she let her jealousy taint our friendship? And how dare she imply that I should take sides? I absolutely refuse to let myself get roped into this "us and them" thing, no matter what Marla or anyone else says. There are people I care about on both sides of this "war." How on earth can I choose between them? Why does everybody in this country have to be so freaking political? Why can't we all just live our lives?

For the next half hour I hung out in my room, waiting for her to call back and apologize. The phone didn't ring.

I went to the kitchen and started getting dinner ready, rehearsing my forgiveness speech while I tossed the salad. But the phone remained frustratingly silent. And it stayed that way for the rest of the evening. By the time I went to sleep later that night, there was only one thought on my mind:

I might just need to find myself a new best friend.

Chapter 24

～～～

Nasir straightened the pillows on the couch and smoothed away the wrinkles in the fabric that were left over from his restless sleep.

Oh, how long have those stains been there? he thought. *And why haven't I ever noticed those rips in the cushions before?*

He grabbed Mama's crocheted blanket from the closet and threw it over the couch. Then he took a step back and tried to see his home as Mackenzie would in just a few short hours. Yes, the couch looked better, but he knew there wasn't much he could do about the rest of the apartment. It was so small — so plain.

What's she going to think of it? he wondered. *She'll know my family isn't wealthy as soon as she arrives. Will it change her feelings for me?*

With a frown, he moved over to the kitchen, noticing for the first time its dingy appearance. He put away his breakfast dishes and then, for the first time in his life, picked up a scouring pad. He squeezed it slightly, feeling the gritty texture against his palm. Then he dropped it down onto the countertop and began scrubbing. It wasn't that the counter was dirty — Mama was too careful a housekeeper for that. But it was dull and old and covered with tea stains, scratches, and Baba's cigarette burns. There were too many to cover up — he had to clean it. But the harder he scrubbed, the duller it became. The call to prayer sounded in the distance. Nasir ignored it and leaned a little harder into the job.

Mackenzie is coming today! Just a few more hours!

Since the minute his family had left town, she was all he'd been able to think about. Inviting her here was a risk, but he had to do it. This would be their first chance to be really alone. He wished he could talk to Ziyad. He'd have some good advice about girls.

Nasir closed his eyes and pictured Mackenzie's pretty face ... her ocean eyes ... her silky hair. He imagined her in his home ... hearing her soft voice and her funny laugh ... holding her hand ... talking ... kissing her strawberry mouth ... making her blush and watching her pale cheeks change into warm roses.

The phone rang. He stopped scrubbing and ran to his parents' room to answer it. It was Mama, calling to see if he'd had a good sleep. He could hear Sameera and Amar chattering in the background and Rana babbling on their mother's hip. Although he missed his sweet little sisters, it was a relief to be away from Baba and, at least for a few days, not have to worry about being dragged out to any late-night digs. Only once Nasir promised to call back after school did Mama let him hang the phone up. When he returned to the kitchen, he stopped in his tracks and stared in shock at what he'd done.

The top layer of the counter was completely worn away.

Chapter 25

After school, I met Nasir at the gates of the Old City. From there he told me it was only a short walk to his apartment. A growing sense of exhilaration took hold of me as we pushed our way through the busy streets of the market. I let Nasir lead the way through the crowds; my head was so dizzy with the prospect of finally being alone with him — *really* alone — that I could barely even pay attention to putting one foot in front of the other.

After walking for about ten minutes, we turned down a small street, ducked under a low doorway, and walked up two flights of stairs to get to his apartment, which overlooked the market. The stairway was dusty and dark and smelled overwhelmingly like cat pee. Even though I tried to pretend that nothing was wrong I was a little grossed out. I had to breathe through my mouth until we got into his apartment — which took longer than it should have because Nasir couldn't find his key. As he fumbled through his pockets, I noticed a pair of dishevelled children lingering in the doorway on the other side of the stairway. Their faces were covered in crumbs and their clothes were tattered and stained. They were staring at me with such intense curiosity that I felt immediately uncomfortable. Nasir noticed them, too.

"She's my ... um ... cousin," he stammered, stepping in front of me to block their view. I looked away quickly, relieved on several levels when he finally found his key and opened the door.

Unfortunately, what I saw inside wasn't much better. I was shocked. I hadn't thought of Nasir as being *this* poor.

I knew the second I walked through the door that there was no air conditioning because the place was very hot and very humid. The floor was covered in peeling grey linoleum, the small countertop was completely worn down, and although the walls were clean, they were chipped and scratched and in desperate need of a new coat of paint. I saw a couple of doors leading off to what I assumed were the bedrooms, but the kitchen, the living room, and the dining area were basically just one large space. It was hard to believe that six people lived here together!

Nasir didn't offer me a tour and I understood why. There wasn't much to see. Aside from a few scattered pieces of furniture and some floor pillows, the only personal items I could spot were a small collection of pictures hanging on an otherwise bare wall. I walked over to take a closer look, eager to learn as much as I could about his family.

There were four photos hanging in a crooked line, each one mounted in a matching gold-painted frame. The first was a wedding portrait taken in black and white. The bride and groom were standing outside in what appeared to be a rose garden. They looked very serious and traditional — so much so that I couldn't tell if they were his parents or grandparents, or maybe even great-grandparents.

The second photo in the line was a baby picture of a little boy. He was propped up on a fleece blanket and dressed in a navy blue sleeper. From one look at the baby's brown eyes and beautiful long lashes I knew right away it was Nasir.

"Aw, you were so cute!" I gushed, pointing to the picture.

"Yes," he whispered, pulling at my hand. Obviously,

looking at pictures wasn't his top priority, but I wasn't finished yet.

My eyes flicked down the line to the third, slightly faded photo. In it, a young boy was holding up a soccer ball and staring out at me with bright, brown eyes.

"Another one of you?" I asked, turning to Nasir.

He shook his head. "No, that's my father's little brother, Anwar. He died during the first intifada, not long after this picture was taken."

I gasped softly and turned back to the photo. This little boy who looked so much like Nasir was dead? Oh my God! I didn't know what to say.

"I'm so sorry," I mumbled stupidly, wishing I could come up with something better. I'd heard those same words so many times after Mom died and I knew from experience how useless they were. Not knowing what else to do, I looked away quickly to the last picture on the wall. It was a family portrait, which I guessed from the lighting and backdrop had probably been taken professionally. I stepped closer to get a better look, and was instantly struck by how beautiful Nasir's mother was. Seated in a chair surrounded by her children, her posture was straight and her head was tilted slightly upward, which made her seem almost regal. She wore a white scarf over her hair, accentuating her smooth olive skin and the delicate features of her face. And her eyes — they shot out from the photo like two black bullets, piercing my own. Something about her gaze made me feel guilty, as if she were accusing me of something. I shifted my eyes to Nasir's three little sisters. They were all very pretty and much younger than I'd imagined them to be. I made a mental note to adjust their ages accordingly in my wedding fantasy. My eyes travelled further up in the photo.

"This is your dad?" I asked, pointing to the tall man standing in the background.

Nasir mumbled something that sounded like a "yes" and tugged again at my hand.

Pushing him away, I leaned forward for a better look.

Mr. Hadad seemed younger than I expected him to be. He had dark brown hair with a few grey threads mixed in and the same café-au-lait eyes as Nasir. I leaned forward and took a closer look, searching for more resemblance to his son. But by this point, my boyfriend had begun to run out of patience.

"Okay, enough with the pictures," he said, taking my hand and dragging me away from the wall. "We came here to be alone."

I knew I couldn't stall anymore. I let him lead me over to a lumpy couch covered in a raggedy blanket. Within seconds of sitting down, his arms were around my back and he was pulling me into a kiss. His mouth was so soft and the moment was so easy and wonderfully private that it made me forget all about the tattered children and the stinky stairway.

"I love you, Muck-and-zee," he whispered into my mouth mid-kiss. I gasped in surprise. As much as I had dreamt about those words, Nasir had never said them aloud before. I considered saying them back when, suddenly, the sound of a key in the lock interrupted the moment. We broke apart just as the door opened and two men walked in.

"Baba!" said Nasir, springing up from the couch. "What are you doing here?"

Baba? Oh my God! His father!

My first instinct was to run and hide, but the apartment was so small there was nowhere to go. My second instinct, believe it or not, was to jump out the window. But I only considered that for a split second before I realized that we were too high up and I didn't want to end up like Marla's cat. So instead, I stared down at my feet and let my hair fall over my face like a veil. My hands were trembling; I was terrified to see what his reaction would be. From everything Nasir had told me, I knew it wouldn't be pretty.

I listened as Nasir stumbled his way through a shoddy explanation.

"Um, this is my, um, friend. We, uh, ran into each other in the souk and came up to get a drink."

I wished with all my might that I could just disappear as I steeled myself for the inevitable explosion. But to my surprise, instead of being angry, his father was apologetic.

"Oh, sorry I interrupted you, Nasir. I ... I had some business to take care of so I left your mother and sisters and came back early. But I see that you're busy. I'll leave you and your friend alone. Please remember your manners and offer her something to eat."

What the hell?

What happened to his traditional parents? The ones that would never approve of him dating a girl before marriage — let alone a *non-Muslim* girl?

I looked up in shock and saw both men staring right at me. I recognized Mr. Hadad instantly from the portrait on the wall. And although I had no idea who the other man was, I was struck with how familiar he seemed. He appeared to be studying my face, but looked away the instant our eyes met. I watched with curiosity as he turned towards the window, leaned his head close to Mr. Hadad's, and whispered something in his ear. Although the words were in Arabic, his voice was just loud enough for me to make out an odd accent. And then, in a flash of panic, I suddenly knew why he was so familiar.

Are you doing some sightseeing? Maybe I can offer you some directions.

Holy crap! That accent, that raspy voice, those empty eyes — it was the man from the souk who had sold me the bowl. One of those black-market dealers Dad said were plaguing the Middle East! My knees suddenly felt weak. I sunk down onto the couch.

Oh, Nasir! Your father's hanging out with a criminal! I wanted to shout. But I held back, scared of saying something in front of this man. Scared of what he would do if he got angry.

What do I do now? I wondered. Should I call the police ... or the Antiquities Authority ... or maybe my father? I thought about the cellphone tucked away in my backpack — the one Dad had given to me for my birthday. Did this qualify as an emergency?

My head was swimming with questions. The only thing I knew for sure was that I had to get out of there. Pulling myself up to my feet, I stood for a second, checking to be sure my wobbly knees would support me.

Nasir obviously sensed something was wrong.

"Are you okay?" he asked, his beautiful forehead crumpling with concern.

I forced a smile and tried to keep my voice from shaking.

"Um, yeah," I lied, "but I really have to go. Thanks for the, um, drink."

Scooping up my backpack, I blurted out a quick "goodbye" and headed back out towards the winding streets of the souk.

Chapter 26

Baba was at Nasir's side the instant the door closed behind Mackenzie.

"That was the archaeologist's daughter, wasn't it?" he gasped, his face shining with excitement. "Did you find out anything?"

For a split second, Nasir was speechless. He had expected his father to be furious at him for bringing a girl home. But then he remembered their conversation in the park.

"Oh, yes, of course it was her. Who else would it be?" he replied, trying his best to sound innocent. He glanced suspiciously over at the man Baba had brought to their apartment. Maybe it was his shifty eyes, or maybe it was the fact that he seemed far too interested in their conversation, but something about this guy made him nervous.

And he liked him even less when he walked towards Baba, snapped his fingers in his face, and asked, "Yusuf, did you just say that girl was an *archaeologist's* daughter?"

The sound of his voice made the little hairs on the back of Nasir's neck shoot up. Although the man spoke quietly, his words were edged with anger — a fact that Baba, however, didn't appear to pick up on right away.

"That's right," he replied, clapping his hands proudly on his son's shoulders. "Nasir met a girl whose father is on staff at The Hebrew University. He's been trying to befriend her in order to help us gain inside information."

Help "us"? Nasir wondered. *Who exactly was "us"? Was I supposed to know this man?* None of this made any sense. He couldn't understand why, after all these weeks of secrecy, his father would be speaking so openly about their "job" in front of a stranger. Bewildered, he examined the man's features, trying to figure out who he was and what he was doing here. He knew from the accent and the way he was dressed that the man was a foreigner. Maybe Spanish or Italian, maybe Turkish — he couldn't tell exactly. But although nothing rang a bell, one thing about his face was obvious: he wasn't happy with Baba's reply.

"An archaeologist's daughter?" he repeated, his voice rising with anger. "Yusuf, you idiot! She saw me — she knows who I am!"

Nasir was in shock. He'd never heard anybody yell at his father before. He wanted to stand up and defend him but he held back, worried it might make things worse. But that happened anyway. With an array of angry foreign words spouting from his mouth, the man turned towards the wall and slammed his open hand against the plaster surface.

Startled, Nasir jumped back — bumping into Baba, who was standing behind him. He felt his father's hands, still on his shoulders, clench with surprise. Perhaps he should have been happy that this man had hit the wall and not them. But all Nasir could think was, *What will Mama say when she comes home to find that huge, sweaty, smudgy palm print on our wall?*

He turned to meet his father's face and communicate a silent question through his eyes: *Who is this guy and why is he yelling at you?* But now it was Baba's turn to look confused.

"What are you talking about, Lino?" he asked the stranger. "How could that girl know who you are?"

"Listen to what I'm saying," the man named Lino ordered, speaking slowly and loudly as if Baba were a naughty child. "I sold her a bowl, an artefact. It was a couple of months ago in the souk — I didn't know who she was at the time. I thought she was just a harmless tourist, not an archaeologist's daughter. Do you see what this means?"

Baba shook his head slowly. "I'm sorry. No, I don't."

Lino growled and cursed again — Nasir could tell he was running out of patience. "It means that she'll tell her father and turn us all in. This is too big an operation to come down because of one girl! If she goes to the authorities and tells them what we've done, everything will be lost. All of my men will go to jail — including you and me ... and your son."

And suddenly, Nasir understood what was going on. This man was Baba's dealer — the one who'd sold their figurine to the rich American. He watched as his father tried to calm Lino down, using the same soothing tone Nasir had heard him use on Baby Rana when she was in the middle of a temper tantrum.

"Don't worry about this — you're just being paranoid. The girl came and left so quickly. She couldn't possibly have recognized you."

"Sorry, that's not a chance I'm willing to take!" Lino replied. And then in a flash he came at Nasir. His hand flew out and grabbed the boy's wrist.

"Do you know which way she went?" he hissed.

"I ... I don't know," Nasir stammered through the pain. "Why?"

"Simple: we must find her and silence her."

"What? No! You can't hurt her," he gasped, the words sticking in his throat.

"Hurt her? Is that what you're worried about?" Lino laughed, although his eyes remained deadly serious. "Stupid boy! Of course I won't hurt her. I'm just going to talk to her and make sure she won't tell anyone about our secret. Now, tell me where she went."

Nasir didn't know what to do. How could he trust this man not to hurt Mackenzie? Panicked, his eyes darted over to Baba, who looked just as frightened as him.

"Please Nasir ...," he begged softly. "If there's a chance she recognized Lino, we have to make sure she won't talk to her father. Who'll support our family if I go to prison? We *can't* get caught."

Nasir looked back at Lino, who was squeezing his wrist so hard it felt like it might snap. The pressure was almost unbearable. *What am I going to do?*

he wondered. *How can I protect Mackenzie and save Baba from jail at the same time?* He closed his eyes, desperately searching his brain for an answer. But that just made Lino tighten his grip even more.

"For the last time, tell me where the girl went!" he demanded.

Nasir's eyes flew back open. "Okay, okay," he said, trying to yank his arm away. "I think she's probably heading towards Bab Sitti Miriam — the Lion's Gate. But if you're going after her, I want to come with you."

"No, you'll stay here," Lino replied, releasing his grasp and pushing Nasir backwards onto the couch. He landed in a heap on top of Mama's crocheted blanket. Before the boy had the chance to catch his breath, Lino took two steps towards him and pulled a knife out from behind his back.

"Now give me her name," he said, pointing it at Nasir's face

"No, I want to come ..."

"Her name!"

"Please, let me talk to her. I know she won't tell anyone ..."

Lino pushed the knife closer. "I need her name!" he roared. "Or, I swear, I'll cut you and your father into pieces."

Nasir heard Baba gasp from across the room. And then his voice began to plead: "I beg you, my son. Do what he says ..."

Nasir took a deep breath and let it out slowly, all the while rubbing the spot on his wrist where, in less than an hour, a large black bruise would begin to appear. He pictured Mackenzie's beautiful face, her white skin, her shy smile. He couldn't let this man hurt her.

"It's M... M... Mary," he lied, hoping that might somehow keep Lino from finding her. Or, at the very least, buy her time to get home safely.

"Mary," Lino repeated, tucking his knife back into his belt and striding across the room. "Come, Yusuf. If we hurry, we can catch her. She couldn't have gone very far."

Baba followed Lino towards the door like an obedient puppy. On his way out of the apartment, he turned to his son and whispered, "We'll be back in a few minutes. Promise me you'll stay here — we'll need you to help sort everything out when we return with the girl."

The door closed behind them with a loud slam. Nasir stared at the grain of the unpainted wood while his mind raced with questions. *What am I going to do? What if Lino tries to hurt Mackenzie? Or hurt Baba?*

How am I going to stop him? Should I call the police? No, I can't — they'll arrest us. Baba can't go to jail! I have to think of another way.

Overwhelmed with panic, he leaned forward and lowered his head into his hands. His fingers clutched and pulled desperately at his hair.

Should I follow them into the market? I could try to run ahead and warn her. But what if Lino sees me? What if that makes him angrier? Then he'll hurt Mackenzie and Baba. I need to think of something else. If they do find her and bring her back, I need a plan.

His pulse was banging in his ears. He shut his eyes, trying to focus his thoughts over the noise. As far as he could figure, there was only one way out of this mess. He rolled off the couch, sunk to his knees, and, for the first time in years, began to pray. Really pray.

Praise Allah ... Give me the strength to do this ... Give me the strength to save Baba and keep Mackenzie safe ... Praise Allah ... Oh please, give me strength ...

Chapter 27

∿∿

I came out of the small side street and looked both ways into the market. For the life of me, I couldn't remember which way I had come from. Did we pass that fruit stand on our way here, or was it the clothing store?

Standing slightly back from the river of people passing by, I looked right and then left, hoping something — *anything* — would jog my memory. But in the end I couldn't be sure; nothing looked familiar.

Hoping it was the right choice, I turned left and took my chances. I figured they were fifty-fifty that I would make it home without getting lost. I also figured this wasn't the safest place to be on my own, but to tell you the truth I was too upset to care. I took a few deep breaths to calm myself down. My mind was still racing with questions.

Should I tell Dad about Mr. Hadad's friend? If I do, will he freak out about the whole boyfriend thing? What's going to happen to me and Nasir? He'd said that the Arab community was close ... Will he still love me if I send his father's friend to jail?

That last question was the most troubling. More than anything I wanted to turn a blind eye to what I had seen and pretend nothing had happened this afternoon. Just keep my mouth shut and not cause any trouble. That's what the old me would have done.

It was tempting, but the more I thought about it, the more I realized that I had no choice. I couldn't let this guy get away with his crimes. To do so would be to betray my *own* father. And I suddenly realized just how much I needed to protect him. The same way he's needed to protect me. I knew in my heart it's what Mom would have wanted us to do for each other.

"I have to come clean and tell him everything," I whispered to myself. Somehow, saying the words out loud made the decision feel that much more final. And in the same breath, I accepted that my relationship with Nasir might very well be over.

The realization of what I was about to do poured over me in a wave of nausea. Stopping by a nervous-looking shoe vendor, I clutched at my stomach in an effort to keep the queasiness from taking over. I breathed in slow, deep breaths, silently willing myself not to throw up all over his table of leather sandals. As soon as the nausea passed, I dug my cellphone out of my backpack and turned the power on.

Suddenly, out of the rabble of the crowd, I heard somebody yelling in English.

"Mary? Mary, wait!"

I spun around and saw Nasir's father running towards me. *Is he talking to me?*

"Mary, wait — you forgot something in the apartment!" he called, pushing his way through the tangle of people. *Yup, he's definitely talking to me. But why's he calling me Mary?*

I watched as he hurried to catch up, his big brown eyes so full of intensity — just like Nasir's. *Gosh, what a nice man*, I thought, wondering how I could have been so scared of him before. Trying to see above the crowd, I stood on my tiptoes and started to wave. But my hand froze when I saw his friend, who was following a few steps behind. I knew from one look at his face that he remembered me. Feeling a little scared, I shook my head and turned to walk the other way.

"Sorry, I really have to go!" I mumbled, hurrying off down the street.

A second later, my entire world turned upside down when I heard the dealer scream something.

"*Wa-ifooha! Wa-ifooha!*"

I couldn't understand the words, but that awful raspy voice of his filled my heart with fear. Instinct took over my body; I started running. The dealer screamed again. I glanced over my shoulder and saw both men running after me.

Oh my God!

Right then and there, the streets of the souk transformed into my own personal nightmare. Panic quickly set in as I crashed my way through the crowded market. I was so terrified I couldn't think straight. I knew why the dealer was chasing me, but why was Mr. Hadad chasing me, too? And where did Nasir go? There *had* to be some kind of rational explanation.

But there was no time to figure it out. Whenever I turned back to look, I saw the dealer's angry, red, panting face getting closer and closer, gaining on me with every step. At this rate, I knew it wouldn't be long before he caught up.

"Help! Help!" I tried to scream as I tore madly through the mobs of people. But I was too overcome with fear to make a sound. I couldn't believe this was happening!

Desperate to lose my pursuers, I turned a sharp corner and quickly ducked into the shadow of a doorway. I held my breath and sent out a silent prayer as the men flew by, passing no more than three feet away from my hiding spot.

Once I saw that they were a safe distance away, I turned around and doubled back. That's when I remembered the cellphone still clutched in my hand. *Thank God Dad programmed his number for me*, I thought, hitting the speed-dial button. But instead of my father's voice, all I could get was a series of loud, angry beeps. I tried again and again, but the phone wasn't picking up a signal. This part of the Old City was a dead spot.

Damn it!

I flipped the phone shut and ran on, stopping for one precious second to grab a scarf from an astonished vendor and wrap it around my hair. I knew my blond, uncovered head had been a spotlight, giving me away at every turn.

Wearing my new disguise, I picked up my pace and kept going. I had a bigger lead this time but I knew it might not last.

Nasir, where are you? my brain shrieked. *Why aren't you here? Why aren't you helping me?* I didn't know what to think. The one thing I knew for sure was that I had to get away from this crazy place and make it home safely to Dad.

I ran and ran and ran, my feet pounding the cobblestones, my pulse throbbing in my ears, my bag hammering against my back with every step. I felt like a fugitive, looking over my shoulder every few minutes to see if they were catching up.

Unfortunately, I was never very good at long-distance running. My throat was screaming with each breath and my lungs felt like they were going to burst out of my chest. I had to save my voice; calling Dad was my only way out of here. Gasping for air, I ran into a small carpet store and ducked down into a dark corner at the back. As my legs groaned with relief, I sunk down onto the floor and tried the phone again. My hands were shaking so badly I could barely push the buttons. *Come on, come on, come on,* I prayed under my breath while my eyes darted around the store. The clerk, a stern-looking Arab man with bushy eyebrows and a red-and-white checkered headdress, was giving me a look like he was about to kick me out any second. And then I heard a ringing in my ear. *Oh my God! A signal!* And then, a second later, a voice.

"Hello?"

It was Dad! I nearly cried with relief.

"Dad? Dad?" I whispered, petrified to give my hiding spot away by talking too loudly. "Can you hear me? I need help!"

"Mackenzie? Honey? Where are you?"

"In the souk — come fast!"

"What? I can't hear you ... Talk louder. Where did you say you were?"

"The Arab souk — in the Old City. Come fast, Dad, please! They're trying to catch me!"

"What are you talking about? Who's trying to catch you?"

I heard footsteps coming towards me and looked up. It was Mr. Hadad and his friend — they'd found me! A wave of panic seized my heart. I screamed so loudly my eyeballs shook. Jumping to my feet, I looked around all the hanging carpets, frantically searching for another way out of the store. Out of the corner of my eye I spotted a half-open door leading to a dingy back alley. I knew it was my only chance. Using every last muscle in my body, I lunged towards it. But the dealer lunged faster. As I hurtled myself into the alley he caught me by the tail of my shirt and pulled me to the ground.

"Dad! Help me!" I shrieked into the phone, which was still clutched in my hand. A second later the dealer grabbed it and threw it down against the cobblestone street, shattering it to pieces ... along with my last chance of being rescued.

Suddenly, I knew if I was going to get out of this mess, I would have to save myself. I remember hearing once that a woman's most powerful weapon is her own voice, so I started using it.

"Let me go!" I shrieked at the top of my lungs. "You can't do this to me! Somebody help! Call the police!"

I used all my strength to wrench myself free from his grasp. I put up the fight of my life, but he was just too strong. Holding me around my waist, he clasped a gross, sweaty hand over my mouth and leaned in so close that the tips of our noses were almost touching. His breath smelled like stale coffee and cigarettes. I wanted to gag.

"Listen to me!" he growled. "If you run or scream again I will be forced to hurt you."

He reached behind his back, pulled out a jagged-edged knife, and held it up to my face. I gasped. Mr. Hadad's big brown eyes stared out at me from the reflection. He looked scared, too.

I turned my head to the left and saw him standing in the doorway a few feet away. Too petrified to make a noise, all I could do was plead with my eyes: *Help me! Don't let this lunatic hurt me!* But he just stood there silently, witnessing my attack. I wondered if his "friend" had threatened him, also.

"Start walking!" the dealer barked, removing his hand from my mouth. Then, with a quick flash of silver, the tip of his knife pointed into the soft flesh between my ribs. I swallowed another scream, terrified he might push it in deeper. He moved the knife around to my back where it would be hidden by the bulk of my backpack. I started stumbling forward, my eyes so blurry with tears that I could barely see my feet.

How is Dad going to find me now? My brain sobbed as I stepped over the remains of my cellphone. *And where the hell is Nasir? Does he have any idea what's happening to me?*

I tripped over a particularly uneven cobblestone and fell to my knees. "Get up," the dealer growled, pulling me to my feet by the straps of my backpack. Then he pushed me forward again — down a maze of alleyways, under a small bridge, up the stinky stairwell, and back to the Hadads' apartment overlooking the market.

Chapter 28

∿∿

Nasir paced back and forth across the linoleum floor. He was so upset he could barely see straight.

"How could you do this, Baba?" he demanded, fighting to hold back his tears. It was hard, but he knew his father would never take him seriously if he started to cry. "Why are you holding Lino's knife? You two promised she wouldn't get hurt!"

He glanced over to the couch where Mackenzie was sitting. A wave of desperation welled up in his chest. She was in the exact place where they had kissed each other so tenderly less than an hour ago. Now, her wrists were tied together with a scarf and Baba was guarding her at knifepoint while Lino made a phone call in the master bedroom. She looked so helpless, so terrified, so confused. Her eyes were filling with tears as she pulled and twisted at the scarf, trying to free her hands. It was killing him to see her like this. More than anything he wanted to go to her, put his arms around her, comfort her, and tell her this was all a big mistake. But he didn't dare. For there to be any chance of getting Mackenzie out of here, he couldn't let Baba or Lino know how much he cared for her.

She looked up from her hands and caught his eye. "Nasir, what are you saying? Tell me what's going on," she pleaded.

He walked over to the couch, but was careful not to touch her. "I'm still not sure yet," he replied, switching over to English. "Are you okay? Did Lino harm you?"

"*Am I okay?*" she repeated. Her voice was quivering with fear, but still her tears wouldn't fall. "No, I'm not okay! My wrists are hurting and I'm scared. Can you untie me? I want to go home!"

Nasir spun around to face his father.

"This is crazy, Baba," he said, lowering his voice so that Lino wouldn't overhear. "That guy is a lunatic! Why are you going along with him?"

Baba sighed loudly and shook his head, keeping his eyes fixed on his prisoner the entire time. "Stop this, Nasir. You know very well why we have to do this.

W-alla! Where is your loyalty? Think of your mother and sisters!"

"Of course my loyalty is with our family," Nasir replied. "But this girl's done nothing wrong." He cocked his ear towards the bedroom and listened. Lino was still on the phone — there was time to get Mackenzie out of here. He clasped his hands together and began to beg. "Please, please, I'm certain she won't say anything to her father! Please, can't we just let her go?"

Baba's gaze flicked nervously in the direction of the bedroom. "Shhhh! No, it's too late for that!"

Seeing her captor temporarily distracted, Mackenzie rose slowly to her feet and took a tentative step forward. Baba's eyes immediately returned to her.

"No! Sit down!" he warned in stiff English.

"Come on, Mr. Hadad," she said, taking another small step towards the door. "Just tell your friend I escaped and everything will be okay."

Nasir held his breath, silently praying Baba would relent. But instead, he darted in front of the door, blocking her way.

"No! Sit down, be quiet," he commanded, waggling the knife awkwardly in her direction.

Mackenzie stared at the blade for a moment, then sat reluctantly back down on the couch. A few seconds later, Lino appeared in the doorway. With the phone still clutched in one hand, he pointed at Baba with the other.

"Yusuf, get in here. We need to talk."

Baba hesitated. "But ... but what about the girl?"

Lino sighed impatiently.

"What's the matter with your son? Is he useless? Let him watch her."

"My son is not useless," Baba replied quietly, handing Nasir the knife. "Don't let her out of your sight," he said, before following Lino out of the room. Nasir nodded, his breath catching in his throat.

This was his chance. He stared down at the weapon in his hands, praying he would have the strength to use it. And use it well.

Chapter 29

~~~~~

Nasir was clutching the knife like a dead fish. Clearly, he had no idea how to hold it. Mr. Hadad and the dealer began speaking in the next room. They were trying to be quiet, but this place was so unbelievably small, we could hear almost everything. Their hurried whispers carried a disturbing sense of urgency. I wished I knew what they were saying. *Damn, all those mornings I wasted studying Hebrew! Arabic would have been so much more useful.*

Frustrated, I turned towards Nasir and begged for some answers.

"Why are they keeping me here? What are they saying? What's going on?"

"Shhhhh," he whispered, holding a cautionary finger to his lips. His eyes were as big as saucers. I'd never seen anyone look so scared.

"You have to listen to me, Mackenzie. We don't have much time," he said, his voice so low it was barely audible. "It sounds like my father is about to leave to find a car. Lino says that he wants to smuggle you into the West Bank."

"The West Bank? Why?" I whispered back.

"He ... he told my father that he knows people there that can make you disappear."

My chest tightened with fear. "What does that mean?"

"I don't know, but I'm not going to let it happen." He knelt down in front of the couch and brought his face so close to mine that the tips of our noses were almost touching. "My father's not a bad man, I swear. He was just doing what he had to do to save our family. And now he's too scared of Lino to let you go. But I'll get you out of here, I promise," he said, his voice little more than a breath on my lips. My heart swelled with hope as he began to unknot the scarf that was wound so tightly around my wrists.

Maybe it isn't too late for us, after all. Maybe when we get out of this place we can just leave Israel together and run away to Hollywood. We can become actors and start all over again in a place with no fathers ... no jealous friends ... no one to judge us and tell us what to do.

The possibility, however remote, energized me. I took a deep, restorative breath and wiped my teary face as best as I could with the shoulder of my T-shirt. But a moment later, everything changed. The man called Lino must have heard us talking, because he suddenly came charging into the room before Nasir had the chance to finish untying me.

"What are you doing? Why are you talking to this girl?" he demanded, his once-empty eyes now full of rage.

I screamed. Alarmed, Nasir jumped to his feet and stood in front of me like a human shield. Although he was taller than Lino, I could see that his physique was too slight to pose much of a threat to a full-grown man. As Lino waited for Nasir to explain himself, Mr. Hadad quietly entered the room. In one hand he was carrying a beat-up duffel bag — a getaway accessory if I'd ever seen one. The top of the bag was unzipped and I could see how it was stuffed to the brim with clothes and maps and ... was that rope?

Heaving the bag over his shoulder, Mr. Hadad said something in Arabic to Nasir. And with that, he left the apartment.

As soon as the door closed, Lino turned his creepy

eyes back on Nasir and me. It was just the three of us now.

"Please," I whispered. "I promise I won't tell anybody what you did. Just let me go home. Okay?"

It was the truth. Let him dig up every artefact in the country, for all I cared! Forget betraying my own dad — at that point I would have promised my first-born child to get away. But unfortunately, he wasn't going for it.

"Shut up! No questions!" he barked.

I swallowed hard and mustered up the last bits of my courage.

"What are you going to do with me?"

"Hey, I said be quiet!" Lino ordered, taking a step towards me.

Nasir moved to block his way. Lino paused, his eyes narrowing.

"Your father was wrong about you," he sneered. "You *are* useless. I saw what you were doing in here. If I can't trust you to watch this girl without trying to seduce her, I'll have to watch her myself. Give me my knife." He reached his hand out to take it back.

What happened next went by in an ugly blur. Hours later, when I tried to recall the details of those minutes, I would only be able to remember the flailing of arms, the flash of steel, and the gush of blood. As Lino reached for the knife, Nasir lunged at him, stabbing his outstretched palm with the tip of the jagged blade.

"*AAAAAHHH!*" Lino screamed, his face morphing with pain. I watched in horror as his blood splattered the linoleum floor in a bright pattern of slick red dots.

"You son of a dog!" he roared, pouncing on Nasir. Ducking out of the way, Nasir managed to slash Lino once more with the knife.

And then the battle ended as quickly as it had begun. Lino grabbed Nasir's throat with his uninjured hand. Nasir's head rocked back. He opened his mouth to scream, but no sound came out — Lino was squeezing his windpipe completely shut.

Oh my God, he's strangling him! What should I do?

I wanted to get up off that couch and tear Lino's hands off my boyfriend. I wanted to save him in the same way he'd just tried to save me. But I was useless as long as my hands were still tied. I pulled at the scarf, trying desperately to free myself as I watched Nasir fight for breath.

With a loud clatter, the knife fell to the floor as Nasir brought both hands to his neck in an attempt to relieve some of the pressure. His whole face was now bright red and his eyes were bulging from lack of air. I stared down at the knife lying only inches from my feet. I knew my only chance to rescue Nasir and myself was to grab it. With my hands still bound, I lunged for the knife. But Lino was faster than me. With a swift motion, he kicked it under the couch.

I turned to retrieve it when a horrible, strangled whine stopped me in my tracks. It was Nasir! I turned back just in time to see Lino pulling him down to the ground, banging his head against the floor in the process and knocking him unconscious. Released from the stranglehold, Nasir lay there on top of Lino's splattered blood. He was frightfully still. Was he alive? I held my breath and waited until I was finally able to detect the slow and steady rise and fall of his chest.

Dear God! He was breathing! He *was* alive, at least for the time being.

But for now it was just me and Lino — who had quickly reclaimed his knife, dashing my last chance at a rescue. My whole body began quivering with terror as my fate suddenly became very clear. He was going to take me to the desert and kill me! My nightmare of a sudden, violent death was about to come true!

While I sat on that couch biting off my beautiful fingernails and waiting for Mr. Hadad to come back with the getaway car, I saw my whole life flash before me — a mental slide show of all the people and places and memories I was about to leave forever.

Birthday parties and Christmas mornings ... dance recitals and camping trips ... first days of school and big family Easter dinners ... learning how to ride a bike, building forts in my backyard, snuggling in my parents' bed during thunderstorms, sleepovers at Christina's house and those late-night Scrabble games where we always ended up falling asleep on the couch.

I saw Mom again in that flashback, so clearly and vividly I swear it was like she was alive again. I saw her brushing and braiding my hair every morning, her mouth full of barrettes and elastic bands. I saw her sitting next to me at the kitchen table, patiently helping me conjugate my French verbs. And I saw her pouring batter into a frying pan as she made those great storybook pancakes while I sat perched on the counter beside her, watching in awe.

But most overwhelmingly, my thoughts were of Dad and the past two years we'd spent together. I saw him camped out in a sleeping bag on my bedroom floor just after Mom died, keeping me company during those first long, dark nights. I saw us doubled over in hysterics in a darkened movie theatre, laughing our crazy-horse laughs at some stupid comedy he'd suggested to cheer us up. I saw us on the whaling excursion we'd chartered on the St. Lawrence, watching the beautiful white belugas frolic in the wake of the boat. And I saw him crowing with pride over my pottery find in Tiberias to everyone who would listen, his eyes overflowing with love for me.

I'd been trying to stay strong this whole time, but something inside me suddenly snapped. I leaned my face into my knees and started to cry. And not a dainty, damsel-in-distress kind of cry ... it was more of the full-out sobbing, heaving, snotty-nose variety. The kind of crying you only indulge in when you're by yourself because it's just too ugly to do in front of anybody else — especially in front of a boy you like. I cried my heart out until my eyes were red and raw and my nose swelled up and my cheeks hurt. I cried hard and hideous and I didn't care. I couldn't remember the last time I told Dad I loved him. And I couldn't stop thinking about how lonely his life would be without me.

All of a sudden there was a knock at the door. I knew it was Mr. Hadad — he must have found a car.

"It's time to go!" Lino growled, grabbing me by the arm and yanking me roughly across the room.

"Noooo!" I screamed, my eyes still blurry with tears. Forgetting about the knife, I swung my bound hands at him, determined to put up the fight of my life. Unfortunately, it wasn't much of a battle. Ducking my fists, he scooped me up and carried me to the door. He struggled to pull it open — trying to balance me over his shoulder with one hand while he yanked on the knob with the other, bloody one. Just as he managed to open the door, there was a sudden, explosive *boom-boom*. I fell to the floor with a painful thud, and then the world went black.

Chapter 30

~~~

"Mackenzie? Mackenzie?"

I opened my eyes and saw my father standing over me, his black cape draped dramatically over his shoulders like a superhero. He was smiling and crying and calling my name.

Did I die and go to heaven?

And then I saw Marla Hoffman emerge from behind him, her normally cool face looking pale and panicky. She glanced down at me, let out a little scream of horror, and covered her eyes.

Okay ... I'm definitely dead!

I raised my head off the floor, searching for signs of my own blood. That's when I saw Lino's body lying next to me. Suddenly I felt dizzy. With a soft moan, I dropped my head back down to the floor. Dad fell to his knees beside me, untied his cape, and threw it over me like a blanket. Then he set to work untying my hands.

"Just lie still for a minute and catch your breath, honey," he said. "I'm worried you might be in shock."

I nodded, so happy to see him ... even if I was dead.

But then I saw the T-shaped tool at his feet. And suddenly I understood. It wasn't *me* who was dead, after all!

"A pickaxe, Dad? You killed him with a pickaxe?"

He looked relieved to hear me talking.

"I was at work when you called and said you were in trouble, so I grabbed the only weapon I could find," he said, picking up my wrist to measure my pulse. "And I didn't kill him, Mackenzie. I just knocked him out with the handle."

As if to prove Dad's point, Lino suddenly stirred and let out a loud, painful groan. I just about jumped out of my skin, petrified that he might be waking up.

Dad was obviously thinking the same thing.

"Oh gosh, maybe we'd better hurry," he said, taking me by the arms and sitting me up. "Do you think you can stand?"

I nodded through the dizziness and let him help me to my feet. That's when I saw my boyfriend's body still lying on the floor by the couch.

"No! We can't leave Nasir!" I said, pulling away from Dad and staggering across the room. I crouched by his side and leaned over his chest, listening for signs of life. His breath was weak, but definitely there. I wanted to cry with relief. But instead, I picked up his hand and gave it a gentle squeeze.

"Nasir? It's Mackenzie — can you hear me?" There was no answer. He remained terrifyingly still — not even a flicker of movement to suggest that he'd heard my voice.

"*Please* Dad," I said, turning around to meet his gaze. "He got hurt trying to help me. We have to get him to a doctor!"

Dad didn't move. He stared at me silently, his grey-blue eyes clouded with confusion. Clearly he wasn't prepared to handle the "save-my-wounded-boyfriend" talk, either. I guess I couldn't really blame him for looking shocked. But right now my concern was for Nasir.

Without waiting for help, I grabbed Nasir under the arms and tried to pull him to a seated position like Dad had done for me. But Nasir was heavier than I'd figured and the effort of lifting him brought the dizziness barrelling back. I swayed on my heels, lost my balance, and fell back down. Luckily, Dad saw it coming and caught me just before I hit the floor.

"I'm sorry, Mack," he said decisively. "But I can't carry *both* of you out of here. He'll have to wait for the police to come. I called them on my way here — they should be arriving any minute."

"But he's innocent!" I wailed. "We can't leave him!"

"Look," he continued, glancing nervously at Lino. "Who knows how many more thugs are on their way here right now. We have to get out of here fast. The police are trained in first aid — they'll take care of this boy when they get here."

From behind us, Lino groaned again, louder this time. Our chance to escape was running out.

"Come on!" Dad said, his normally calm voice growing urgent. "We're leaving right now, even if it means I have to carry you out of here kicking and screaming!"

I didn't want to abandon Nasir, but I knew Dad was right. What else could I do? I had no choice but to leave my boyfriend on that dingy linoleum floor. I leaned on Dad's shoulder as he helped me to my feet a second time. That's when I spotted Marla still lingering in the doorway. She couldn't seem to take her eyes off Lino. There was an intense frown of concentration on her face, like she was working on a geometry problem or something. Suddenly, she pointed at the body and yelped.

"Holy cow, Mack! I think that's the guy from the souk who sold you the bowl!"

"What?" Dad cried, taking a closer look at the man he'd just pickaxed in the head. "What are you doing in *his* apartment?"

This time I didn't need to see his face to sense his confusion — it was coming across loud and clear in his voice. I tried to explain as best as I could in my frazzled state of mind.

"I ... I just found out today that he's Nasir's ... that is, um, my boyfriend's father's friend. He was going to kill me."

Dad gasped. I know that was hard for him to hear. His grip on me weakened and, for a split second, I worried that he might drop me back onto the floor. But a moment later, he shored himself up and called for Marla.

"Come on, pick my cape up and wrap it around her shoulders. Then help me get her out of here."

As he and Marla led me out of the apartment, we passed the crooked line of photos hanging on the wall. My eyes connected with Nasir's photograph and my guts twisted with guilt. I couldn't help wondering what was going to happen to him and his family now.

With Marla holding up one side of me and Dad holding up the other, the three of us made our way down the smelly stairwell and back through the souk. We moved as fast as we could, considering that they pretty much had to carry me most of the way. It wasn't until we jumped into a taxi that we finally felt safe enough to talk. That's when the details of my rescue came out.

"So, how on earth did you know where to find me?" I asked as the cab careened around a corner and sped away from the Old City.

Dad steadied himself against the back of the passenger seat and nodded over at Marla.

"Don't look at me …," he said.

"What?" I turned to look at my friend … the same friend I was ready to disown less than twenty-four hours earlier. "How?"

They exchanged glances. "Do you want to tell her or should I?" asked Dad.

Marla looked a little embarrassed. I swear, that must have been a first for her.

"You go ahead and tell it," she said.

"After you called I was desperate to find you," he explained. "You said you were in the souk, but that's a mighty big place to search. I phoned Marla, praying she'd have an idea where you were. That's when she told me what you'd been up to and brought me to the apartment."

I stared at Marla in surprise.

"I don't get it — how did you know where Nasir lived?"

"I kind of followed you there earlier this afternoon," she said, looking down at her hands.

My mouth dropped open with shock. "You did? Why?"

"After we talked last night, I knew you were getting in way over your head with this whole thing. I wanted to see where Nasir was taking you and make sure you were okay. I guess I feel responsible for you, Mack — kind of like your big sister or something. Anyway, once I saw you guys go into his apartment, I went home. I knew you had your cellphone if you got into trouble. And I couldn't exactly follow you inside, could I?"

"No, I guess not," I agreed, although I wished she had. Then maybe I could have avoided this whole mess.

"So," she continued, "the phone was ringing when I walked in my door, and of course, it was your dad. When I heard about your phone call, I brought him back there right away. And that's when we found you. From the looks of things, I guess we got there in the nick of time."

She paused for a second as her olive eyes filled with tears.

"See? I told you this would end badly, didn't I?" she added, her face crumpling with sadness. "*God, Mack!* They killed my mother and they almost killed you, too."

And then she started to cry. Those words had ripped the Band-Aid off what was clearly still a raw wound. How could I have been so stupid? *Now* I finally understood why Marla never liked Nasir. I'd gone and misjudged her just as terribly as she'd misjudged him.

"Mar," I said softly. "I know losing your mom was devastating — she didn't deserve to die. But you can't blame every Arab for her murder. Nasir didn't kill her. And neither did his father or anyone else from his family. The person who killed her was an angry radical. Nasir was trying to save my life."

Suddenly, the driver veered sharply to the right to avoid another car, smacking my body up against the vinyl wall of the cab. That's when I started crying, too — actually, it was more like sobbing. After

all I'd been through that day, you might not think I
had any tears left. But there they were, pouring down
my cheeks fast and furious, creeping into the corners
of my mouth until I was forced to swallow the bitter taste of my sadness. I felt doubly ashamed — for
leaving Nasir behind, and for the way I'd treated my
best friend.

"I'm so sorry," I whimpered. "You had my back
and all this time I thought you were ... well, jealous ...
You know, of me having a boyfriend and all." I cringed
to hear myself say those words. I'd been so self-ab-
sorbed and petty. How could I have so totally missed
what was really going on?

Marla's eyes widened with surprise at my confes-
sion. "Jealous? Me? No, I was never jealous. Just suspicious ... and scared ... and I guess a bit neurotic.
That's what happens when a suicide-bomber rips your
life apart."

The air in the cab suddenly felt as hot and close as
it had in the Hadads' apartment. Gasping for breath,
I rolled down my window and let the wind rush over
my face. The cab driver glanced over at me. He looked
nervous, like he thought I might self-destruct right
there in his back seat. I just ignored him and kept
crying. The wind blew some of my sadness away and

helped dry my tears. After a minute I felt a bit better. I took a long, shuddery breath and patted my friend's shoulder softly.

"All right, I'll stop crying if you will, okay?"

"Only if you say you don't hate me for telling your dad about you and Nasir."

"I could never hate you," I sniffled, giving her a hug. "And thanks."

She hugged me back. "S'okay. I'm just so glad you're all right."

And that's how good a person Marla Hoffman was. Right then and there I knew that I'd never consider replacing her as my best friend again.

I was quiet during the rest of the cab ride. I couldn't stop thinking about Nasir. Was he on his way to the hospital? Did the police arrest Lino? What about Mr. Hadad?

As desperate as I was to find out, I had no choice but to push those questions to the back of my head. The trauma of the day was definitely catching up with me — what I needed most was my bed and my Frou-frou.

After we stopped at the police station to file a report — which took forever — we dropped Marla off at her apartment building and went home. You can't even imagine how great it felt to be back in a place I thought I'd never live to see again! Dad tucked me into bed with a cup of peppermint tea and my beloved bear. I was so exhausted I thought I'd fall asleep right away. But I tossed and turned for a long time, thinking of Nasir. Did the police get there in time? Was he safe? His voice kept echoing in my head, saying "*I love you, Muck-and-zee*" over and over. And all I could think was how I never got the chance to say it back.

Chapter 31

I woke up the next morning to see Einstein camped out in a sleeping bag on my bedroom floor.

"Dad?" I croaked, sitting up in bed. "What are you doing here?"

He rolled over and opened his eyes.

"Hey, good morning."

Then, with a stretch of his arms, he opened the sleeping bag and came over to sit at the foot of my bed.

"I couldn't sleep last night, thinking about you alone in here. I had to make sure you were safe, so I snuck in here in the middle of the night. Hope you don't mind."

"No, I don't mind," I replied, reaching for Frou-frou.

He folded his arms across his chest and took a deep

breath. When he spoke again, his voice was low and serious. "You gave me quite a scare yesterday, Mack."

I hung my head. "Yeah, I know. Sorry, Dad."

"What were you doing in that boy's apartment, anyway? You were dating him behind my back?"

Oh God! Time to face the music.

"Um, yeah ...," I admitted sheepishly. There was no point trying to cover it up anymore.

Dad cleared his throat and began tapping his foot on the floor — two sure signs that he was not pleased. I knew if he started rubbing his forehead, big trouble was definitely coming.

"And how long has it been going on?"

I sighed and picked at the fluff balls on Frou-frou's one remaining ear. "A few months. I wanted to tell you, but I knew you'd just make me stop seeing him."

He looked hurt. "How can you be so sure about that? We could at least have talked about it."

"Come on, Dad! You wouldn't even discuss the idea of dating at all. Remember my birthday?"

The old "pin-stuck-in-the-butt" look flashed across his face.

"Yes, I remember. But the whole idea just made me nervous. I want you to be safe, that's all."

I sighed again, then slumped down on my pillow. "I understand, Dad, but you're treating me like a child, and I'm *not* one anymore!"

"I do not treat you like a child," he protested.

"Please! Who else but a ten-year-old has a seven o'clock curfew?"

He paused and began rubbing his forehead. Horns from the intersection below filled the silence while I waited for his reaction. But when he spoke again his voice wasn't angry at all. In fact, it was a little hoarse.

"You're right, honey. I guess I've been kind of out of it for a while ... probably since Mom died. You seemed like such a little girl when that happened and now, well ... I just don't know what to do with a young woman."

I was shocked to hear him admit that I was a young woman, and even more shocked to hear him bring up Mom ... He never did that! My heart softened a bit when I saw the tears in his eyes; I could tell this was difficult for him.

Before he could change the subject, I took a deep breath and asked, "Dad, do you ever wonder what Mom would have thought of it here?"

He paused for a second and dabbed at the corners of his eyes with his fingertips. When he spoke again, his words caught in his throat.

"Y-yes, I do. All the time."

I dropped Frou-frou and reached for his hand. It felt rough compared to the soft fur of my bear. But it was warm and just as familiar. I gave it a light squeeze.

"And?"

"I think she would have adored it. I think she would have soaked up the history and culture of this place. She would have loved the dig in Tiberias. I thought about her a lot when we were there. I know how fascinating she would have found the whole process — even though she didn't have any formal training, she was always an archaeologist at heart."

I smiled at that. After Tiberias, I felt that way, too.

"But I think the thing she would have loved most about this place would have been watching how it affected you, Mack."

I was surprised by that. "Me?"

Dad nodded. "You've become a different person since we moved here. You're more confident, more independent. You're definitely more assertive. I think — no, I *know* Mom would have been proud of you."

Tears stung the backs of my eyes. I didn't reply. I just let those words sink into my heart.

Mom would have been proud of you.

Chapter 32

∿∿

Later that morning, a tall, lanky policeman came to our door. I immediately recognized him as Detective Stern, the officer who'd taken my statement at the department the day before.

"Good afternoon Professor Hill ... Miss Hill," he said with a couple of cordial nods of his head. "I have some news about your case. May I come in?"

I could tell from the low tone of his voice and the deep furrow between his brows that, whatever the news was, it wasn't going to be good. A jumble of knots began to form in my stomach as Dad stepped aside to let him in. Once we were all inside the apartment, Detective Stern pulled out his notepad, cleared his throat, and promptly proved me right.

"*Ahem*. So the officers we dispatched to the Hadad residence arrived approximately fifteen minutes after you reported leaving. Although blood was found on the floor, the perpetrators had apparently fled the scene."

"Excuse me," Dad interjected. "What do you mean they 'fled'? Both of those men were badly injured."

"I mean that the apartment was empty," the detective replied, looking up from his notepad.

The knots in my middle began to tighten. "S-so, where did they go?" I asked.

He frowned, and the furrow in his forehead grew even deeper. "Well, that's exactly what we're trying to find out, Miss Hill. After an intensive search of the building, the market, and most of the surrounding neighbourhoods, our officers turned up no trace of them. Wherever they went, it appears that they were able to cover their tracks quite well. In fact, considering the nature of the injuries that you reported they sustained, we suspect that these guys must have had some help."

He paused for a moment to let this information sink in, then turned towards me and said, in a voice that oozed suspicion, "Miss Hill, we were hoping that perhaps you could shed some light on the matter. You mentioned yesterday that one of the perpetrators," here, he glanced down and began flipping through his notepad, "a minor named Nasir Hadad, is your boy-friend?"

Oh my God! What was this guy implying? I could feel my face begin to burn with an angry heat. Suddenly on the defensive, I spit out a reply.

"Yes, he is my boyfriend — or, he was ...," I paused briefly. "But he definitely wasn't a perpetrator — he was a victim, just like me. And no, I don't know where he went. You're the detective ... did you check the hospitals?" My voice cracked on the last word as I remembered the horrible image of Nasir lying unconscious on that floor. I felt like crying again. But Detective Stern didn't look like he cared much.

"Yes, of course we did," he said curtly. Then he let out a loud, frustrated sigh and slapped his notebook closed. "Look, you're probably a nice kid who just got mixed up with the wrong guy. So I'm going to cut you a break here and give you a second chance."

I glanced over at Dad to see if he knew what this guy was talking about. But he looked just as confused as me.

"A second chance?" I asked. "At what?"

With his hands on his hips, the detective leaned down and peered directly into my eyes. I swear, it felt like he could see right through my pupils and straight into my head. He spoke slowly, enunciating every word so there would be no misunderstanding.

"Look, you're a foreigner here and obviously you have no idea what you've gotten yourself involved with. But if you're protecting this boy, I promise you'll be in serious trouble — the kind of trouble your consulate won't be able to help you out of. So what I'm asking is simple: would you like to make any changes to the official statement you gave me yesterday?"

A bubble of silence filled the room while he waited for my reply. But I couldn't speak. Instead, I just stared at him in shock. *Holy crap, is he accusing me of hiding Nasir?* I didn't know where to find the words to answer him.

Thank God Dad stepped up and spoke for me.

"We appreciate your offer, Detective Stern, but Mackenzie will not be accepting it. Thank you for coming out today."

I could hear the controlled anger in Dad's voice clipping away at his words. Detective Stern must have heard it, too. He stood back up to his full height, smoothed down his shirt, and spun around to leave.

"Thank you for your time, Professor Hill," he said on his way out the door. "You'll be hearing from us soon."

My whole body sagged with relief to see him go. After that, I made a promise to myself: I was going to find Nasir on my own. Maybe it was stupid, but I really thought I could do a better job than that smarmy detective.

I spent the rest of the day calling around to all the Jerusalem area hospitals looking for Nasir. But Stern had been right on that point: none of them had a patient by his name registered in their care.

And so, after school, I walked over to the little hole-in-the-wall corner store. It was the first time I'd been back since a couple of days ago when Nasir had invited me to his apartment. God, that felt like a lifetime ago!

I walked in the door half-expecting to see his beautiful, smiling face waiting for me behind the cash register. But for the first time ever he wasn't there. Instead, I was astonished to find an overweight, balding man standing in his place. I wondered if this was Mr. Khoreibi, the man Nasir told me had hired him.

"Good morning," the man beamed, clearly pleased to have a customer. But when I asked about Nasir, his big smile disappeared.

"That lazy goat?" he sneered. "He hasn't shown up for work in two days! When you see him, tell him to get his skinny butt back here!"

I left the store in a hurry, trying to figure out where to look next. All I could think about was finding Nasir.

You know, I'd never really considered the term *heartbroken* before. But after losing both my boyfriend and my mother, I knew it was a totally inadequate way to describe the feeling of overwhelming pain ripping away at my insides. *Heartbroken*: it was just too neat. A round, red heart severed neatly down the middle by a clean, jagged line. *Heartsmashed ... heartdemolished ... heartsquashedtoapulp* ... any of those would have been better ways to describe the feeling. Except this time around, the hardest part had to be grappling with the unanswered question: was Nasir alive or dead? At least when I lost Mom, I had that information. Not knowing was pure torture. I kept wondering if I'd ever see him again.

I decided to head back to the souk. Of course, I couldn't tell Dad where I was going — he'd never have allowed it. But I knew I had no choice if I wanted to find Nasir. The Hadad family had lived there, after all — there *had* to be somebody there who knew where they'd gone.

Pushing my fears aside, I went back to the Hadads' apartment, only to find the doorway blocked with police tape. I tried speaking to the landlord of the building, but his English was too shaky to tell me anything. In desperation, I went to a camera shop and had an enlargement printed of my secret, wallet-sized photo of Nasir. I spent the rest of that day and every day after school for the next two weeks wandering up and down the souk with the picture in my hands and a question on my lips: *Have you seen this boy?* But in reply, all I got were blank stares and silent, shaking heads. If anybody had seen him, they weren't saying.

After three weeks of searching I gave up. It was as if Nasir and his whole family had disappeared off the face of the earth. I forced myself to face the awful truth: the time had come to start mourning my first love.

Chapter 33

Within a couple of months, the school year came to an end and Dad and I found ourselves packing up to go home to Canada. Remember when I was nothing more than a grumpy tagalong to Dad's plans? By the end, I was begging to stay. Despite the bad stuff that had happened, Israel felt like my *real* home now. I didn't think I had anything left in common with my old friends in Toronto.

But just like the first time, Dad said "no."

"Sorry, honey, but we've given up the apartment. Besides, I have to use the summer to get ready for the coming year."

When I asked if I could stay with Marla's family for the summer, his answer became even more emphatic.

"It's just you and me now. We're all we have left in this world and we have to do things as a family.

When you're eighteen, you can make your own decisions about where you want to live."

It was almost word for word the same speech I'd heard a year before. But this time around, it didn't make me angry.

This time around, it actually made sense.

The day before our flight, Dad announced that there was one more thing we had to do before we left Israel. "There's a place I've been meaning to take you," he said. His blue-grey eyes flickered with secrets. I was intrigued.

"Okay, where?"

He shook his shaggy head. "No, no — don't ask questions. Just put on something demure like a long skirt and let me surprise you."

It was a strange request, but I decided not to argue. I loved a good surprise. But an hour later I was a bit disappointed when we ended up back in the Old City.

"This isn't new, Dad. We've been here a million times before," I complained.

"Just come with me," he replied, throwing an arm around my shoulders. He took me through the Armenian quarter, down a series of long, narrow, cobblestone paths, until we came to a steep stairway. I have to admit, I was a little confused. There we were in front of the Western Wall again — the same spot we'd come to on our first tour of the Old City.

"Why here, Dad?"

He smiled. "I promised I'd bring you back again one day, didn't I?"

My mind skipped back to that day last July when we were fresh off the plane, when this city seemed like a foreign planet, when I was still so angry at him. We'd passed by the Wall wearing tank tops and shorts.

"*Next time, we'll bring better clothes,*" he'd said.

Aha! So that explains the skirt.

Before I could ask another question, Dad took my hand and began leading me down the stairs. At the bottom, we went through a metal detector and then stopped in the giant open-air plaza in front of the Wall. There were huge crowds of people milling around us — people quite clearly from all different areas and walks of life. There were old people ... young people ... light-skinned people ... dark-skinned people ... men in suits ... hippies in tie-dyes ... black-hatted rabbis ... camera-toting tourists ... armed soldiers ... security police ... tiny new babies ... hunchbacked grannies ... and, of course, me and Dad.

And in front of us all loomed the Wall — tall, heavy, and daunting. In the area right in front of it, a dividing fence separated the male visitors from the female.

"Hey, why are they separated?" I asked, pointing to the fence.

Dad leaned over and whispered, "I believe it's considered immodest for men and women to pray together."

"Oh."

We watched in silence for a few minutes. It was a fascinating scene. The air was thick with the melodious sing-song of Hebrew prayer. Most of the men were swaying and rocking as they prayed. And when they were finished, they walked backwards away from the Wall to avoid turning their backs on the holy site. Remembering Professor Anderson's advice, I was careful not to make eye contact with any of them.

"Look carefully between the cracks of the stone, Mack, and tell me what you see," said Dad.

I squinted until I was able to make out what looked like paper stuffed in between the massive sand-coloured bricks.

"Tsk. What's all that? Are people littering here?"

Dad laughed at that. "No, far from it. Those are prayers. For thousands of years, people have written their greatest hopes down on paper and pushed them into the cracks of the Wall."

I looked at him like he was crazy. "Why?"

"This is a sacred place. So sacred that many believe that the gates of heaven are situated directly above it. And they also believe that putting their prayers in the Wall is one of the surest ways of communicating with God."

Gates of heaven? Images of St. Peter and angels and harps suddenly sprang to my mind. I glanced up at the sky, but all I could see up there were a couple of thin wisps of cloud and some circling birds.

"Anyway, I guess that's the reason I brought you here today," he continued. "I know we've never been at all religious, but I thought if you had a message or something you wanted to send out into the universe, this would be a good place to do it."

I hesitated. "Um, I don't know, Dad — I'm not sure what I would write."

He pulled out a small notepad from his back pocket and tore me off a sheet. Then he handed me a pen and said, "Take your time and think about it. I'll be over on the men's side. Meet me back here when you're done."

And then he walked away. Suddenly I was nervous.

"Wait!" I called after him, jogging over to catch

up. "What are *you* going to write?"

He shook his head. "Sorry, but that's kind of private — sort of like a birthday wish. All you have to do is write what's in your heart."

I grabbed his arm.

"But are you sure we're allowed to do this? I mean, we're not Jewish."

"Don't worry, people of all backgrounds and religions pray at this wall. Pope John Paul II was here before his death, putting his own prayer in the cracks. It's one of the holiest spots in the world."

"Come on, Dad," I begged, like a little kid pleading for a toy. "Help me. What should I write?"

"Relax, honey. You don't have to do this if you don't want to. Just remember, there's no right or wrong thing to say."

And with that, Dad walked over to the men's section of the Wall and left me alone with my thoughts.

I stood there for the longest time, staring down at the notepaper in my hand while the crowd ebbed and flowed around me. My mind was a total blank. I wasn't used to saying prayers or talking to God. But Dad said "write what's in your heart." So I closed my eyes and tried to figure out what exactly that was. When I opened them again, the words were there.

Squatting down, I tore the paper into two pieces and wrote on the first half:

> Dear God, please forward this to Elizabeth Hill:
> Mom, I miss you so much. Don't worry about me and Dad. We're going to be okay.
> Love you forever, Mackenzie

I put it into my skirt pocket and wrote on the second half:

> Dear God, please watch over Nasir, wherever he is.
> And please tell him that I loved him too.

Tucking it next to the first note, I walked over to the women's section — which, by the way, was *way* smaller than the men's, something I didn't think was fair at all. But since nobody else seemed to be complaining, I stayed quiet.

Feeling a little bit nervous, I pushed my way through the crowd of women — teenagers, young mothers, little girls, and old ladies, all of them layered in so much clothing that only their hands and faces showed. The old ladies in particular looked like they'd been there forever. Parked on patio chairs and covered all in black, they seemed like permanent fixtures, weeping and wailing as they prayed. I weaved my way around them until I was right up next to the Wall.

Reaching out tentatively, I ran my fingertips over its ancient, bumpy surface. From far away it had looked so big and imposing, but up close it was soft, light, and smooth — almost friendly, like a colossal sandcastle. Maybe it was because it was covered with dark, mossy plants, but the Wall seemed alive, somehow. And there was an energy in the stone that made me feel welcome.

My eyes skipped over the surface, slowly taking in all the notes that had been stuffed into each and every crevice. There were hundreds — no, thousands of them — crammed into the cracks, pushed in so tightly they had become as much a part of the Wall as the ancient stones that surrounded them. So many prayers, so many hopes, so many messages — it took my breath away. I wanted to read them and see what others had written, but of course, I didn't.

Instead, I took my notes out of my pocket, folded them into two small squares, and reached up high to stuff them into one of the emptier cracks, pushing them in with my fingertips until I knew they wouldn't fall out. Then, resting my hands on the stone, I looked up again into the blue desert sky, searching for ... I'm not quite sure what. A sign of heaven? A sign of God? A sign of Mom? I didn't see anything, but it didn't really matter. I felt good, like I'd finally written the goodbyes I'd never had the chance to say.

A minute later I walked away through the crowd of women and went back to find Dad. Not long ago, the sight of all these mothers and daughters would have made my heart ache with sadness. But not today.

I guess maybe I *have* changed.

Acknowledgements

~~~~

Writing a book is never a solitary endeavour. I'd like to thank the following people for their help: Gordon and Shirley Pape, for a lifetime of support and encouragement; Jordan Kerbel, for his limitless love and devotion and for affording me the luxury of pursuing a career in the arts; Jonah and Dahlia Kerbel, for those golden stretches of rare silence that allowed me to work on this book; Simone Spiegel, for inspiring this story and generously sharing her wealth of personal memories; Marsha Skrypuch, for believing in me, pulling me out of the writer's dumps, and pointing me in the right direction; Martha Martin, for her invaluable insights and advice; and Natalia Buchok, for sharing her knowledge and experience of Israeli-Arab culture.

I'd also like to thank the uber-talented group of writers on the online kidcrit literary forum for their outstanding critiques. And, lastly, I'd like to thank my valiant agent, Margaret Hart, and the wonderful team at Dundurn, especially Barry Jowett, for working their magic and breathing life into Mackenzie Hill.

RECENT RELEASES FOR YOUNG PEOPLE FROM DUNDURN

She Loves You
by Rhonda Batchelor
978-1-55002-789-1 $11.99, £6.99

Locksmith
by Nicholas Maes
978-1-55002-791-4 $11.99, £6.99

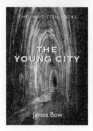

The Young City
The Unwritten Books
by James Bow
978-1-55002-846-1 $12.99, £7.99

Snakes & Ladders
by Shaun Smith
978-1-55002-840-9 $12.99, £7.99

www.dundurn.com

Available at your favourite bookseller.

Tell us your story! What did you think of this book?
Join the conversation at www.definingcanada.ca/tell-
your-story by telling us what you think.